THE PEABODY–OZYMANDIAS TRAVELING CIRCUS ODDITY & EMPORIUM

F. PAUL WILSON

FOREWORD

All this started with a book called *Freak Show.*

Freak Show was one of three theme anthologies contracted by HWA to put itself on firmer financial footing. Rick McCammon, Ramsey Campbell, and I were chosen as Editors. Rick's *Under The Fang* came first and was a disjointed collection of vampire stories with the premise that the undead have taken over – now what?

I was up next. I spent the early months of 1990 mulling a theme and a structure for my anthology and decided on a traveling circus / freak show. I boned up on circuses and such (in *libraries,* folks – no Google back then) and talked to Harlan Ellison about his experiences when he ran away from home at age 13 to join a circus but wound up in a freak show, and Dean Koontz about his sources for *Twilight Eyes.*

And while I was doing this, Bob Weinberg called in April, asking for a story for the 1990 World Fantasy Convention program book. As writer GoH that year, I was expected to contribute some original fiction. Well, I was knee-deep in circus lore, so why not use that setting? And since Bob's wife Phyllis was the world's number-one Repairman Jack fan at the time (the only Repairman Jack fiction extant in 1990 was *The Tomb* and the novella,

"A Day in the Life") I decided to write a Jack story and dedicate it to Phyllis.

Thus, "The Last Rakosh" is the first appearance of Oz and his troupe.

On May 30, the first 20 letters went out to the biggest name writers I knew personally and felt I could work with. I wanted *Freak Show* to be more unified than *Fang*, so I included three pages of guidelines outlining the background of Oz and company, and how my connecting story would run, plus the general circular route the show would take around the country.

I asked for a description of each writer's freak and an outline of the story. This was necessary to avoid duplication of characters, locations (I didn't want three stories in Chicago or LA) and plot lines. It also pretty much guaranteed that once I approved a proposal, I'd buy the story.

Many of the invitees – including Stephen King – turned me down. A number said they found the guidelines too restrictive; others blasted off and came up with great stories. I opened it then to the HWA membership and was inundated.

After the synopses were set, I began tying them together – solidifying an overall story arc and adding interstitial material to link the individual pieces. I also circulated descriptions of all the freaks to the contributors to encourage cross-fertilization (a passing mention of this freak or that in other stories).

This took a year of my life and interfered with my own writing projects. But I was 90% satisfied with the outcome.

The paperback, published September 1992, was truly ugly and disappeared very quickly – yet has become something of a collector's item. I've done a number of online searches and can't find a copy for less than eighteen bucks. Borderlands Press did a hardcover limited edition signed by all contributors, and I can't find a copy of that for less than $75.

Fine and good. That was that. Until 1998 when I incorporated "The Last Rakosh" into *All the Rage.* This got me thinking about Oz & Co. again and wishing my story and interstitial material were available to my readers. After all, it was linked to the Otherness and the Adversary Cycle.

But I was too busy to cull out my sections and rewrite them into a presentable whole with no prospect of finding a home for it. (It would never be novel length, and back in those days the small presses were publishing only novels or fat anthologies and collections.) So the idea lay fallow for more than a decade until Don Koish approached me and asked if I'd write a novella for his Necessary Evil imprint. I wanted to – I'd been blown away by his deluxe edition of Tim Lebbon's *Dead Man's Hand* – but had no time for anything new.

However...

We made a deal. I took my original *Freak Show* material and fleshed it out, adding new characters and situations. In the process it wound up fifty percent longer than what I'd started with. I called it *The Peabody-Ozymandias Traveling Circus & Oddity Emporium.* The 500-copy Necessary Evil Press edition sold out before publication and is almost impossible to find. Readers have been requesting a reasonably priced edition. So… since I like to see my work remain in print…

…here you have it.

I hope you enjoy the journey.

F. Paul Wilson

The Jersey Shore

Fall 2008

NB: For those interested in interconnections, the story takes place about a year or so after *All the Rage,* in the summer before *Nightworld.*

PART ONE
WINTER QUARTERS

OKEECHOBEE COUNTY, FL

1

"Freaks?" Joseph Peabody said. "In my show? That's asking a lot. A *lot.*"

The crusted bowl of his briar felt warm against his palm as he struck a wooden match to it and befogged his immediate vicinity. Ashes sprinkled the latest issue of *AB* lying open on his lap. He eyed his visitor through the blue-white smoke.

Jacob Prather's son—Ozymandias. Weird name, that. Almost as weird as the fellow it belonged to. Well, Jake hadn't been too tightly stitched himself. Joe had known him when they were both with Taber & Son's mud show. Joe had been assistant manager and Jake had had a gig in the sideshow—some sort of weird machine that didn't do nothing, just sat there and looked strange. Nice enough fellow, but Jake got decidedly weird after his son was born. Finally quit the circuit just about the time Joe had got together the wherewithal to buy Taber's failing show and rename it after himself.

Peabody's Traveling Circus—he'd match it up against any other two-tent mud show in the country for giving a family its money's worth when they bought a ticket.

Joe never saw Jacob Prather again. And now, years later, here comes his son, back in the business.

The circus does have a way of getting into your blood.

Ozymandias Prather looked nothing like his father. Jake had been a small, stoop-shouldered, bespectacled field mouse. His boy was tall—six-five, maybe. He didn't stand, he *loomed.* Lank dark hair, parted on the side and plastered down; pale skin, lips so thin his mouth looked like a skin crease, and blue eyes as warm as a mausoleum. A funny-shaped body: His shoulders were narrow, his arms long and thin, yet he was barrel-chested, with a broad but paunchless abdomen set upon wide hips. His head was normal-sized but his torso made it look too small for his body. The overall effect distorted perspective. Even looking straight at him Joe had a feeling he was standing in a hole looking up.

"Why should you want to refuse?" Ozymandias said in a deep voice that seemed to come from everywhere in the room but his lips.

Joe shook his head. "A freak show . . . that sort of thing's never been my style. You should know that. As a matter of fact, it's *out* of style."

"Gawking at the deformed is never out of style."

Joe sensed bitterness there—a *load* of bitterness.

"I don't know, Ozymandias—"

"Most people find it easier to call me Oz. You've seen my troupe, Mr. Peabody. If you don't think they can turn the tip, then you're not the showman I think you are."

"Yeah, I've seen your troupe," Joe said, repressing a shiver. In all his sixty-six years he'd never seen such a collection of oddballs. "Where on earth did you find them?"

The razor-thin lips curved upward at each end. A smile. Sort of.

"Diligence hath its rewards. But that is irrelevant. An offer is on the table: cash up front for a forty-percent interest in Peabody's Traveling Circus. Your only concessions are to add my name to the logo and put a few extra stops on the route card, but you retain control. A can't-lose proposition for you."

"I don't know about that. My people aren't going to like it." Peabody's general manager, Tom Shuman, and manager, Dan Nolan, were up in arms about even the possibility of sharing the stops with a bunch of freaks. "We run a clean show. We've got a reputation—"

"But you're losing money and you're almost broke. I've seen the balance sheets, Mr. Peabody. My troupe can bring in the extra crowds, the people who think high-wire acts and waltzing elephants and clowns and foot juggling are passé. They'll come to see us, but they'll stay for your show, and they'll buy our flukum and popcorn and balloons and T-shirts."

"I want no grift," Joe said emphatically, and he meant it. "No games, no monte, no prostitution."

He saw Oz stiffen.

"I have never allowed that in my troupe. And I never will. We don't need grift to turn a profit."

Joe believed him. Something in his gut warned him away from the man, urged him to throw Ozymandias Prather out on his ass, but he sensed a Puritanical streak in this oddball and believed he'd run a clean show. And the hard truth was the show was looking Chapter 11 in the eye. Ozymandias Prather was offering a way out. And at least Joe would still be in control.

Reluctantly, he held out his hand.

"You've got a deal, Oz." They shook. Oz's hand felt cold but dry. "I'll have my lawyer draw up the contract. By the way, any idea what we should call this new conglomerate?"

Oz rose and towered over him. His bass voice boomed.

"The Peabody-Ozymandias Traveling Circus and Oddity Emporium."

"Quite a mouthful, but being such a mouthful just might make it work. By the way, how's your father?"

"Dad? He killed himself years ago."

Oz then stepped out the door, leaving Joseph Peabody alone in his chair, sucking on a dead pipe.

2

Outside the trailer, Oz stood under the stars and closed his eyes a moment. He wanted to celebrate, wanted to guzzle champagne and shout his elation. But he had work to do.

As if on cue, a tall, lean figure separated itself from the shadows. An exquisitely handsome face, dead pale, with cold, cold eyes, leaned into the light.

"He accepted?" said Tarantello in a voice as dark and silky as his tailored black suit.

"Of course. He has no choice."

"A lot of money."

"What will money mean if we're successful?"

Tarantello nodded. "And so it begins."

"And so it ends," Oz said. "For all of *them.* Drive me back and have the Beagles bring the players to the meeting tent."

"Everybody?"

"No. Just our kind."

3

George Swenson sat in his trailer trying out a new glue for his suckers—he'd developed a rash from the old stuff—when a sudden pounding on the door made him spill the glop all over his left arm.

"Damn! What is it?"

He heard a growl from the other side and knew it was one of the Beagles. Daubing at the glue with a damp rag, he crossed to the door and wrapped his sticky arm around the knob. He hadn't had a chance to replace it with a lever and it was damn hard to turn a knob when you didn't have fingers. Finally he twisted it far enough to slip the latch.

One of the Beagle Boys stood outside, pointing across the clearing toward the meeting tent. George didn't bother trying to figure out which one this was. Impossible to tell. The Beagles were identical quints, five muscle-bound hulks, virtually neckless, with tiny ears, close-cropped hair, deep-set eyes, and toothy grins. All were mute but managed to get across what they wanted you to know, even if they had to get rough to do it.

"A meeting? All right. I'll be there in a few minutes."

The Beagle held up a meaty fist. The message was clear: Don't forget, or else.

"Yeah, sure," George said, undulating an arm at him. "I'll be there."

Then he slammed the door.

George didn't know what to make of Oz's entourage. Some of them had been together for years, traveling the South and occasionally venturing up the East Coast. George was a newcomer, a "first of May" in the lingo. Oz had come to him a couple of months ago at the very nadir of his twenty-two-year life—out of college due to lack of funds, out of work because no one wanted to hire a guy with boneless forearms that looked like tentacles. Oz offered him a job.

Not a great job. In fact the worst job imaginable—a sideshow freak. He glued flesh-colored rubber suction cups to the underside of his tapered, handless forearms and *presto!* He glanced at the poster on his wall.

Octoman!

The Human Octopus!

Product of an Unholy Union between

Woman and Sea Monster!

Yeah, right. His mother had never even seen an ocean and his father had been a car salesman. The closest George had ever been to a carnival before this was when his mother would take him as a child to the Taber & Sons show on its annual trip through Moberly, Missouri. She'd loved circuses and sideshows. She'd gone every year before he was born and saw no reason to stop after. He'd gawked at the bearded lady and the pinheads, giants, and dwarves, never dreaming that one day he'd be a gawkee instead of a gawker.

Dwarves, giants, bearded ladies, pinheads . . . they were Rotary Club next to this troupe. Yet for all the sinister shapes and bitter, suspicious attitudes, George had felt an instant kinship with these . . . freaks.

God, he hated that word, but what else could you call them? They were freaks of nature. Unassimilable accidents who didn't belong, who had nowhere else to go, who were fit company for no one but each other.

Luckily George wasn't like them. He had a future. He was going to finish college, get his degree in computer science, and go on from there. He'd be so damn good at systems analysis no one would give a rat's ass that he had no hands.

He finished wiping off the glue and headed for the meeting tent. Something had been in the air about joining up with a mud show for a long summer tour. Maybe Oz had struck the deal.

4

"It will be a long trip, brothers and sisters," he said as he walked among the members of his troupe. "Long in distance and in days."

Half an hour ago Oz had watched them straggle in and seat themselves in a rough circle. He'd hurried through the mundane details of the coming tour, and now he segued into the important part, the crucial part, the part they would have difficulty grasping and believing.

"And perhaps it is good that we make a full circuit of this country—better yet if we could make a circuit of the globe—for it will allow us a chance to see it and remember it as it was—if we care to."

He let his gaze range over them as he allowed the words to sink in.

All the important ones were here. The special ones, the ones like him. Three-eyed Carmella sat with melon-headed Leshane Burns, flashing sidelong glances at George Swenson who sat alone; the bovine Clementine also sat alone, but not necessarily by choice; woody-skinned Bramble sat near green-skinned Haman who appeared to be staring at the closed tent flap while the eyeless Gerald Gaines stared at nothing yet saw every-thing; Delta Reid coiled around her chair as Janusch waved his stalked eyes about. Others sat scattered about. The troupe had no unity yet. They were not yet a team. But they would be by the end of this tour. They'd be *family*.

Tarantello hovered at the rear while the Beagle Boys manned the flaps—this was a *private* meeting.

The troupe. The freak show. People with green skin, white skin, furry skin, reptile hide, no eyes, extra eyes, no digits, extra digits, people with visions, with no vision, with one face, with two faces. A gathering to give many a townie nightmares for life. But to Oz they were beau-tiful. Because they were kin. Brother and sister were not forms of address he took lightly. Truly *kin*. For they shared a common parent, a *third* parent that had left an indelible imprint on their genes.

The Otherness. Each had been touched by the Otherness.

George Swenson looked up at him from under a furrowed brow and posed the question Oz had known someone would ask.

"Remember it 'as it was'?" he said. "I don't get it."

"I shall explain," Oz said. "But first I must tell you that I did not arrange this tour merely to make more money. We will do that, but the money is unimportant." He watched the brothers and sisters nudge each other and mutter. He'd expected that. "What is important is the search. For while we are touring we will be searching for a series of objects."

"Like a scavenger hunt?" Janusch said, his eyes standing tall.

"In a way, yes. But in this hunt there will be no single winner. If we are successful, *all* of us will be winners."

"What will we win?" George said.

"Justice. Understanding. Acceptance. Compensation."

The expressions facing him—the readable ones—were frankly dubious.

"I don't get it," said Carmella, blinking her third eye.

"And you never have," Oz said. "Justice, that is. None of you has. You've been shunned at best, and at worst you've been reviled, abandoned, beaten, and tortured. But never . . . *never* understood. With your cooperation, this tour will change all that."

"Will it give me hands?" said George Swenson.

"No," Oz said. "You won't need them."

"Will it give me arms?" said Earl Cassell.

"No. You won't need them."

"Will it straighten my spine?" said Ginny Metcalf.

"No. You won't need a straight spine."

"Will it let my branchlets live for more than a few minutes?" said Bramble.

Oz smiled and nodded. "Most definitely yes."

"Will it get me a keg of German beer?" said Leshane.

Everyone laughed.

"I still don't get it," said Delta.

"A change," Oz said. "We have an opportunity to work a change upon the land. And the instrument of that change cannot be activated until we find all its components and reassemble them."

"A *machine?*" George said. "A machine is going to change the world?"

Oz nodded. He'd known this was going to be a tough sell. He barely believed it himself. But he had to have their cooperation. He could not succeed without it.

"Yes. When the Device is activated at the proper time in the proper place, it will, quite literally, change the world—change the way the world sees us, change the way the world sees *itself*."

He paused and let them mutter among themselves, then raised his voice.

"You need not believe me. I realize that might be too much to ask. But I do ask that you trust me. As we make a circuit of the country I will from time to time ask one of you to venture into the town we are passing through and retrieve one of the missing pieces of the Device. You do not have to believe that it will change our place in the world; all you need know is that it is important to me and to those of your brothers and sisters who do believe."

Oz turned in a slow circle, eyeing each in turn.

"Have I ever lied to you?"

He noted with satisfaction that every head was wagging back and forth.

"No. I do not lie." He pointed to the outer world beyond the tent wall. "*They* lie to you. I do not. And I say to you now that the Device is monumentally important to all our lives. Is there any one of you who will not help collect its component parts as we travel?"

Oz searched the members of his troupe for a raised hand. He saw none.

"Excellent. And to give you some idea of the nature of the Pieces you'll be seeking, I've brought along a few to show you."

Oz withdrew the four objects that had been waiting in the pockets of his coat and handed them to the nearest members of the troupe.

"Here. Pass these around. Don't worry about damaging them—you can't. Just don't lose them."

5

George felt something like a cold shock when the first Piece reached him. The sensation ran through his boneless forearm up to the left side of his face; from there it seemed to penetrate his skull and shoot across his brain. Vertigo spun him and for an instant he thought he saw another place full of weird angles superimposed on the tent space—*coexisting* with the tent space—then he steadied again.

He looked down at the thing in his hand, blinked, then looked again. Dull yellow metal, but such a strange shape. A couple of the sides met at an angle that didn't seem possible—shouldn't have been possible.

He passed it on and reached for another.

This one looked hard and glossy but felt soft and fuzzy, almost alive; he thought he sensed it breathing.

He quickly dumped that one off and reached for the next—a flat ceramic oval.

But he sensed something wrong with this one too. He couldn't pinpoint it at first, then he noticed it didn't cast a shadow; it was solid, opaque, but no matter which way he turned it . . . no shadow.

The last object was a tennis-ball-size sphere and it did cast a shadow—but one with sharp angles.

George cradled this last Piece in his coiled left arm and stared at Oz where he stood in the center of the tent. One strange dude. Aloof and yet paternalistic; even the freaks who'd been with him for years knew little about him. He'd heard more than one mention that no one had ever seen him eat. Full trays were delivered to his trailer and removed empty, but he always ate alone. His only close contact seemed to be Tarantello, another one who never seemed to eat—never even got trays. The freaks kidded about taking "a walk with Tarantello." George didn't know what that meant but decided from the timbre of their voices that he'd rather not find out.

And now these Pieces. Strange little things to say the least. Almost . . . otherworldly.

One could only imagine the sort of Device their aggregate would produce. An instrument like that might be capable of almost anything.

Even Justice . . .

. . . Understanding . . .

. . . Acceptance . . .

. . . Compensation.

6

Oz stood with Tarantello and watched the tent empty.

Tarantello said, "Do you think they'll ever believe?"

"Some will be a tougher sell than others, but when the time comes, they won't have much choice."

"They're used to not having much choice."

Oz glanced at Tarantello whose debonair exterior hid his particular deformities. Because of that, he could move unnoticed among the hoi polloi. And that was important, for it allowed him access to sources of the Fuel. Oz had discovered the distilling technique in one of his ancient tomes. He'd taught Tarantello, and the man proved to be a master. The Fuel was crucial. Without it Oz would not be able to keep his promise to the troupe.

As he pocketed the Pieces he'd displayed, he glanced right and saw George Swenson standing beside him. George offered the end of his tentacle-like right arm. Oz shook it.

"Very moving," George said. "I want you to know you can count on my help if you need it."

"That's good to know, George."

"Of course, your Device will be more important to the others."

"Really?"

"Yes. I'm sure once I get enough money together to finish my education I'll be able to get by on my own. But I'd like to help the others. So just let me know what I can do."

"Thank you, George."

As George moved out of earshot, Tarantello whispered through a tight smile.

"Is our first-of-May also the Eternal Optimist?"

Oz watched him go. "He still thinks of himself as one of *them*."

"You going to tell him the whole story?"

Oz shook his head. "Like so many of the others, George isn't ready for it."

"Want me to think of a way to make him ready?" Tarantello said, his smile widening.

"Yes. Do that. Come up with a way to convince him that he will never be accepted by them, that we are his real family. And his only hope."

7

Joe listened to Tom Shuman's rant.

"Never thought I'd live to see the day," Tom said as he stood at the door of the office trailer and stared at the cluster of new trailers and campers parked across the field. "Joe Peabody touring with a freak show. Who'd believe it?"

Joe looked up at his general manager. Tom had an angular body and a reedy voice. He handled the circus's performers and Joe had known there'd be a ruckus when he found out about the freak show. He'd been dreading this moment.

"All a question of dollars and cents, Tom. We tried all winter to raise the operating capital we needed for this year's tour. Couldn't get it. Not in this economy. So it's a choice: Tour with them or disband the show. Which do you prefer?"

Shuman tossed his cigarette butt outside and turned toward the desk.

"You know the answer to that. But mark my words, there's gonna be trouble."

"There's already trouble," said Dan Nolan, a burly, muscular hulk in the chair near the inner corner of Joe's desk. "A buncha my roustabouts took one look at those freaks this morning and blew the show."

Nolan was his other manager, in charge of the workers.

"Get some more," Joe said.

"Hey, I combed every mission, homeless shelter, and Salvation Army office in the county to come up with these bums. Nobody wants to work."

"I have workers, Mr. Nolan."

Joe started at the voice echoing through the office. Oz loomed in the doorway. Joe introduced him to Tom and Dan. No one shook hands.

"I don't want your workers, mister."

"How do you know that if you've never met them?" Oz said. "I'll call them."

He turned, raised a silver whistle to his lips, and blew. Joe heard nothing, but a moment later, five burly figures crowded around the door. They were identical, all stamped out with the same cookie-cutter—neckless, deep-set eyes, pug noses, and toothy grins.

"The Beagle Boys, Mr. Nolan. They follow instructions and don't talk back. And they're *very* strong. They're yours when you need them. Give them a try."

Grumbling that he didn't have much choice, Dan slipped past Oz and confronted his new roustabouts.

"Go with Mr. Nolan, boys," Oz said. "And do what he tells you." Then he stepped inside next to Tom Shuman and looked down at Joe. "What's the route so far?"

Joe reached into his desk and pulled out the route card.

"Let's see. So far we've got fifteen dates across the Deep South and Southwest in late May-June. A dozen stops on the Left Coast in July, ten across the Midwest and into the Northeast in August, then we'll make the home run down the East Coast in September. Hopefully, we'll pick up more as we go."

Oz handed him a sheet of paper. "Here are some extra stops I wish to add."

Joe studied the list of locations. Some they were already booked into or near, others were pretty far out of the way. But rather than get into it now, Joe temporized.

"I'll see what we can work out."

"Excellent." Oz reached into his coat pocket and pulled out a foil sack. "And here's something for you."

Joe took the proffered bag and unrolled the top. An exotic aroma wafted up from within. For an instant it made him almost giddy.

"Tobacco?"

"A gift. A special mix from India. I think you'll like it."

"Why . . . thanks." The unexpected gesture took Joe by surprise. "Very kind of you."

"Enjoy."

Oz waved and was gone.

"Trouble," Tom Shuman said, staring after him. "Nothing but trouble."

Joseph Peabody lit a bowlful of the new tobacco and drew a few tentative puffs. He felt lightheaded again for a moment, then it passed. Strong, but smooth. An unusual flavor. He had a feeling he was going to like this blend.

"You worry too much, Tom," he told his general manager. "I've got a feeling we're going to have the tour of our lives." He drew another mouthful of rich, sweet smoke from his pipe. "My, this tobacco is good."

PART TWO

ON THE ROAD

GLASCOCK COUNTY, GA

1

The show rolled.

Up through the northern Florida counties, breaking in the firsts of May, getting the kinks and bugs out of the acts in the tiny towns, playing big in Jacksonville, then sliding across the Georgia line into Charlton County.

Along the way an artist named Caniglia latched onto them, saying he wanted to sketch the freaks. Oz thought the experience might be amusing to the troupe and so he let him travel along. Caniglia was quiet, soft spoken, and promised not to get in the way.

When the show stopped in Moniac on the edge of the great swamp, Oz called Earl Cassell into his trailer. He had a job for him.

Earl had no arms to speak of. But he had toes. Oh my, did he have toes. Sixteen of them, brown gnarly things varying in length from one inch to an extraordinary seventeen. The troupe called him—surprise—Toes, but the public knew him as The Amazing Monkey-Footed Man.

Hard gray eyes stared at Oz from a weather-beaten face.

"There's a Piece in this town," Oz said as he offered a Xerox of a drawing.

Earl took it with his left foot and held it before his face, studying it.

"Who drew this?"

"That is not important." But it was. The artist had been Oz's father. "What is important is that you are uniquely fitted to retrieve it."

Earl flexed his tangle of toes. "Really."

And then Oz pulled out a map and showed him the mangrove patch where he'd find it.

Earl shook his head. "Easier to find a needle in a haystack."

Oz smiled. "But this won't be just any needle. This one will call to you."

Looking dubious, Earl shrugged and shuffled out of Oz's trailer.

He doesn't believe, Oz thought. But soon he will. Soon.

2

"Another pair of workers blew the show last night," Nolan said.

Joseph Peabody puffed his pipe and watched his manager prowl the office, sporting the red bandanna he affected when they were on the road. Workers blew the show every season. Most were winos, drifters, petty criminals, or all three in one. They slept on bunks stacked four high in smelly converted semi-trailers, spent their off time guzzling Mad Dog, and usually did their work with blistering hangovers. Always more where they came from. Why was Nolan so worked up?

As if sensing Joe's question, he said, "It's those freaks."

"Got enough men to get the top up when we get to Athens?"

"I've got enough *bodies* to do it. Those Beagle Boys . . ." Nolan shook his head. "They're striking the tents now and . . . Jesus, they're strong. Work as hard as the bulls."

"Then what's the problem?"

"They make my skin crawl—that's the problem. And the animals ain't too fond of them neither."

"As long as we get the canvas up and down, and the lumber moved in and out, go with it, Dan. The crowds have been good so far. Oz's folks are bringing them in. If these first two weeks are any indication of how the season's going to go, we'll be looking at the biggest end-of-tour bonus we've seen in ten years."

"No kidding?" Nolan's dour expression mellowed a bit. "All right. I'll make do with what we've got left."

"I'm counting on you, Dan."

When Nolan was gone, Joe sighed and repacked his bowl. He'd hired Dan to oversee the workers and Tom

Shuman to nursemaid the performers, but he in turn had to nursemaid Nolan and Shuman. He lit his pipe. He'd grown quite fond of this new blend from Oz. Each bowlful offered a quiet pool of tranquillity amid the hustle and turmoil of the tour.

A tap on the door. He looked up, saw Ginger, and smiled.

"You wanted to see me?" she said.

"Come in, come in. I always want to see my favorite niece."

How true. His sister Rosemary's daughter was damn nice to look at. Sweet face, sweet figure, sweet heart. Blue eyes and red-gold hair that Joe swore his sister must have seen before she named her. A little headstrong, a tendency to pout, but cute as a bug.

Joe hadn't wanted Ginger in the circus, but Rosie had been an aerialist in her youth and had infected her daughter. A spot for Ginger had been part of the deal when Joe had hired the Fugazis a few years ago. She'd worked out fine.

Ginger wrinkled her nose as she sat down.

"Something wrong?" Joe asked.

"Is that your pipe tobacco? Smells strange, like . . ." She seemed to run out of words.

"I know what you mean. I can't identify it either. But it tastes wonderful. Anyway, I called you here to tell you what a good job you're doing. I watched you in the

Spanish web last night and you were perfect. And your trapeze act with . . . what's his name? The Fugazi boy?"

"Carlo."

"You two work very smoothly together, like you've been doing it all your lives."

"He's a good teacher."

"Glad to hear it. Just wanted to let you know I'm proud of you, and keep up the good work."

Her smile was sunlight as she waved at the door. "Thanks, Uncle Joe."

3

Ginger was feeling pretty good about herself as she walked through the backyard. Her mom had tried to discourage her, Uncle Joe hadn't wanted to hire her, but she'd hounded the hell out of them and here she was, aerialist with the Fugazis. Skill and hard work had a lot to do with it, but so did luck: The younger generation of Fugazis was almost entirely male and they needed a certain number of women for their act.

The roustabouts had the tents down but some of the older performers were still hanging around the backyard, sitting on lawn chairs and jackpotting. Ginger loved to listen to their tales of the old days on the kerosene circuits along the back roads of the South, but she had no time for that today. She had to get her trailer hitched up and ready to roll.

She was passing near one of the animal trucks parked in the shade when she noticed a young man sitting on a picnic bench with Neely, the circus's new baboon. Neely didn't seem to know she was a monkey. Rather than be lonely and pining for a fellow baboon, she'd decided she was human and hung out with humans at every opportunity. She liked everybody and everybody liked her. She would groom anyone who sat near her and loved to be groomed in return.

Ginger hadn't seen the young man before. He seemed about her own age. He sat hunched forward, elbows on thighs, hands between his legs as he let Neely groom his hair. He was kind of cute. She noticed his muscular shoulders and back—not iron-pumping bulk, but lean, sleek, hard-work muscles. Neely was working her long fingers through the dark blond hair that curled over his ears and down the nape of his neck to the collar of his Nickelback T-shirt.

She considered that neck: clean. With bathing limited to bucket baths, you didn't see many clean necks in the circus. Though worn, his shirt was clean too. She liked him already. But when he turned and smiled at her over his shoulder, when she saw his pale blue eyes and bright, warm smile, something tugged within her chest and she caught her breath. He was gorgeous.

"Hi," he said. His voice was like his face—light, open, friendly. "I hope Neely's not finding anything."

"Doesn't seem to be." Ginger stepped closer. His hair was clean, glossy. Obviously he took good care of himself. "She doesn't need to. I think it's some kind of ritual with her."

"I only wish I could return the favor."

She leaned forward and stroked Neely's fur.

"That's easy. All you've got to do is—"

At first she thought he was exposing himself, or playing with himself, or something equally sick. Then she noticed that the smooth fleshy tube wasn't rising from his fly, but was attached to his arm. In fact it *was* his arm. Both of them tapered gracefully to long, curving, prehensile . . . things . . . ropes . . . *tentacles.*

The sight of those twisting, coiling arms came as an icy slap in the face. All the rising warmth she'd been feeling plummeted through the hole that ripped open in the bottom of her stomach.

She'd been about to ask him if he'd just joined the show but the question was unnecessary now. She'd avoided the freak tent and had stayed away from the freaks' section of the backyard. The whole idea of deformed people putting themselves on display repulsed her. And here was one now, right in front of her, making a fool out of her.

She spun and hurried away.

4

George felt an aching void form in his chest as he watched the girl's retreating back. He'd seen her before, watched her bikinied form in rapt wonder night after night from the back door of the big top as she did her spins and poses on the vertical rope of the Spanish web, and her graceful, vaulting glides from trapeze to trapeze. He even knew her name: Ginger Cunningham. And just a moment ago she'd been standing not two feet from him, speaking to him, smiling that beautiful baby-faced smile—

Until she'd seen his arms.

George had long ago stopped being self-conscious about them. After four years as a high school gymnast, a foreshortened year as a college gymnast performing in front of crowds of all sizes, and a couple of weeks now of displaying himself as Octoman, he'd doubted he could ever feel self-conscious again.

But he realized now he'd been wrong. The way her eyes had widened, the way her smile had withered into a tight line of revulsion, he'd felt . . . naked. He glanced around. No one seemed to be watching. No one except Tarantello, who met his eyes for a second then turned and sauntered off.

George stood and pulled away from Neely. He gave her a quick stroke along her back, then headed for his trailer. Despite the heat he felt a sudden need for a long-sleeve shirt.

Wilcox County, Alabama

1

The pounding startled George. He removed his iPod earpieces—cutting off Kate Bush in mid-note—and looked at his trailer's only door.

What the hell?

The pounding came again. The wet back of George's T-shirt peeled from the backrest of his easy chair as he reluctantly left the cooling gusts of his electric fan and stepped to the door.

He found one of the Beagle Boys standing at the base of the pair of steps, silhouetted in the light of the high, bright moon behind him. He pointed through the night toward Oz's trailer, gesturing him to follow.

"What now? Another gathering?"

The Beagle only growled and repeated his gestures.

George sighed and stuck his iPod in his pocket. Might as well go see what Oz wanted. If he didn't go on his own, he had a feeling the Beagle would drag him.

He made sure to lock his trailer door. He'd learned the hard way not to leave anything lying around. The lowlifes working for the circus would grab anything that wasn't nailed down. It was almost expected. And whenever anything went missing, "the Bear" always took the blame.

Can't find it? Sorry, can't help you. The Bear musta got it.

He followed the Beagle's hulking, moonlight-limned shadow through the still, sodden air. He missed his fan already.

He found Oz waiting for him beside his old Lincoln Town Car.

"Get inside, George," he said in his rumbling voice.

A request or an order? Either way, it startled George.

"Me? Where are we going?"

"I'll explain along the way."

George eyed the big, black idling car. Something sinister about it . . . like it should have had a funeral home's name on the side.

"I don't know . . ."

"It's air conditioned."

"Okay!"

He pulled open the passenger door and reveled in the frigid flow from within. With a sigh he slid onto the seat and slammed the door.

Heaven.

Oz seated himself, shifted into gear, and got them rolling toward town.

"Before you ask again," the big man said, "we're going to church."

George hadn't been prepared for that.

"I don't get it."

Oz swiveled his head to offer a mirthless smile. "A propitious choice of words, George. That's just what we're going to do: Get it."

"Get what?"

"A Piece . . . one that is now part of a Councilville church."

George felt a wave of uneasiness. Going to a church, on a Thursday night? That could only mean . . .

He shook his head. "I . . . I told you I'd help you, Oz, but I didn't mean I'd help you steal them."

A rumbling laugh. "If I wanted to steal it, I'd have brought along one of your brothers instead—one better equipped for the task."

Oz's brothers-and-sisters talk didn't sit well with George. Never had.

"I'm an only child, Oz."

Damn straight. After seeing him, his parents had sworn off children. Probably swore off sex as well.

A big hand reached out and gripped George's shoulder. "But you're not. You have an extended family right here with us. I want you along tonight as a step along the path to your accepting that."

George said nothing.

Related to Haman . . . or Delta Reid? He couldn't— didn't want to— imagine it.

2

"Who is it?" said a weary voice from behind the closed door.

Oz said, "Someone who must speak to you, Father Putney."

"Just a minute."

As he and Oz waited, George looked around. What were they doing here? Councilville was a sleepy little town in the Cahaba River basin that seemed to have put itself to bed early. They'd driven straight to this Catholic church and parked in the pocked, weed-stubbled lot. Saint Lucian's itself seemed fairly new, at least in style. But even with the full moon as the only illumination, George sensed a sad shabbiness about the place. The planting beds needed weeding, the bushes needed pruning and removal of the kudzu overgrowing many of them; the church's trim could have used a fresh coat of paint as well.

Instead of approaching the church, they'd crossed the parking lot to this little ranch house. A sign by the door read *RECTORY*. It was in the same sad shape as the church.

Finally an overhead light came on and the door opened a few inches before being halted by a chain lock. A pudgy face with watery blue eyes and wire-rim glasses peered out at them.

"Good evening, Father," Oz said. "Remember me?"

"How could I forget? You were here last year. Well, let me tell you, the answer is the same. You can't buy the window."

"But as I told you, Father, I don't want the window, merely one small, insignificant piece of it."

"Sorry. The answer is still no."

The door started to close but suddenly a *thud!* boomed through the night as Oz lashed out with his right foot. It sprang open with enough force to break the chain lock. The priest staggered back, his terrified eyes bulging.

"Help! Hel—!"

Oz's speed surprised George. He was upon the priest in an instant, cutting off his cries with a long-fingered hand around his throat.

"I did not come here to hurt you, priest, but I did not come to be dismissed like some door-to-door sales-man either."

When George recovered from his shock, he noticed that the priest's skin was purpling, his Porky Pig face swelling even further with trapped blood.

"Oz!" He wrapped an arm tip over one of his boss's shoulders. "Don't you think you should loosen up a little?"

Oz ignored him and pulled the priest closer. "We're taking a walk over to your church. You can come silently or I can drag you by your throat."

Then he released his grip but kept his hand poised to resume it.

Coughing and gagging, the priest said, "I'll come."

"Good. Bring your keys and let's go."

The priest pulled a key ring from a hook by the door, but as he turned back his gaze came to rest on George's arms.

"Saints in Heaven! Who's he? *What* is he?"

"Your better," Oz said.

He took the priest by the back of his neck and propelled him from the rectory. Once outside, Oz glanced at the moon.

"Keep moving. We haven't much time."

Time for what? George wondered.

But he said nothing. Anxious, he looked around, turning in a full circle as he searched for signs of life.

What if someone saw Oz pushing the priest around? What if they called the cops?

He hated this. He wished he hadn't come.

As Oz marched the priest across the almost day-bright parking lot, he said, "How's your parish doing, Father? Thriving?"

The priest glanced at him. "Since I assume the question rhetorical, I won't bother answering it."

Oz turned to George. "Years ago, Saint Lucian's was a thriving parish with an active, enthusiastic membership. Then a storm damaged the stained-glass window over the entrance. A local artisan was commissioned to repair it. Since some of the glass had been shattered beyond repair, he went searching for substitutes. I covet one of the stand-ins he used. It was originally part of the collection I am rebuilding. I told you about my collection, remember?"

George nodded. "A Piece is in the church window?"

"Yes." They were approaching the front steps. Oz pointed above the entrance. "Right there."

George looked up, expecting the traditional rosette. Instead he saw a large rectangle, perhaps three times wider than tall. He couldn't make out the design, but something red seemed to glow near its center. The Piece?

The priest unlocked the door and led the way inside. But as he reached for the light switch, Oz grabbed his wrist.

"No lights. You can only appreciate this in the dark."

Again his fingers took hold of the back of the priest's neck and propelled him into the center aisle of the nave.

Father Putney's voice quavered. "I don't understand."

That makes two of us, George thought.

"Tell us, Father, what has happened to your parish since you had your stained glass window repaired?"

"Why, nothing. Nothing at all."

"Are you in denial, or are you lying? Your membership has dwindled, your collections have fallen below the level where they'll pay for even minimal upkeep. And it's not that the parish dislikes you. If that were the case, they would be traveling to other towns to join other parishes, attend mass in other churches. But that's not the case, is it, Father."

"The town has fallen on hard times and—"

Oz jerked him to a stop midway along the center aisle.

"Lie to yourself, but don't lie to me! Your former parishioners have not migrated to other parishes. And do you know why? Because they've lost their faith."

"No! Not all of them! I can't believe—"

"Believe! And I'm about to show you why." He turned and pointed to the sanctuary. "Watch."

George turned too. Moonlight filtered through the stained glass window, bathing the altar, the pulpit and the flanking statues—St. Joseph to the right and the Virgin Mary to the left, her arms cradling the baby Jesus, her feet crushing the serpent of Evil. And behind them all hung a huge crucifix.

The priest said, "I don't see . . ."

"You will. What you will see happens only twice a year, so I was not able to offer a demonstration on my last visit. Tonight is one of those occasions: the night of the full moon nearest the solstice."

George turned and looked up at the wide window over the balcony. Through it he saw the bright disk of the moon inching toward its center. The window depicted a longhaired man dressed in a white robe. A halo hovered above his head. St. Lucian, most likely. He held a book in one hand and a scepter in the other. Half a dozen figures, many holding open books as well, knelt on either side. George gathered that Lucian must have been some sort of theologian or church scholar.

But the most striking aspect of the mural was the clear red stone at the head of his scepter. It glowed especially bright as the moon crept behind it.

The Piece . . . it had to be the Piece.

"George," Oz said. "Take this and go up to the balcony."

George looked and saw that Oz had produced a hammer from somewhere.

"But—"

"Go up there and wait. Don't worry. You won't miss a thing. You'll have a bird's eye view of what is to come."

George knew with a sinking feeling that Oz was going to tell him to break the window and grab the Piece. He could land in jail for that—the last thing he needed.

But he wrapped an arm tip around the handle and trotted toward the rear. He found the stairway and hurried to the top—just in time to see the Piece focus the moonlight and beam it into the church, bathing it in red light.

Red . . . yet not red . . . not like any other color he'd seen, a hideously beautiful shade, at once attractive and repellent. It struck a chord within, a strange resonance. The light had an odd, shifting quality, as if reflecting off invisible coiling shapes along its path. He traced those coils to the sanctuary and gaped in awe as the statues began to change.

St. Joseph's lips twisted into a demonic grin as his hands began stroking a huge erection that had sprung through his robe. The Virgin also smiled, a fanged smile, crimson with blood from the torn throat of her infant. The freed Serpent wound around her thigh to lap at the infant's drippings. A many-legged creature lay twitching and bleeding on the altar, a sacrifice to a nameless god. And the crucifix . . . the huge crucifix had been inverted; the Christ figure was gone, replaced by a writhing, slug-like creature nailed in its place.

The priest's scream of revulsion echoed from below.

The phantasm lasted no longer than a minute. As the red light faded, so did the images, allowing the sanctuary to return to normal.

George saw the priest turn to Oz and raise his arms.

"Blasphemy!" He swung his fists but Oz grabbed his wrists and easily restrained him.

"Perhaps," Oz said, his voice calm, almost cold. "Perhaps not. But either way, it is your doing."

"Mine? Are you mad?"

Oz pointed to the window. "Look up there. That red piece in your window, the one you refused me, is the cause. What you just witnessed occurs twice a year. It is brief in duration, but its aftereffects linger. When your parishioners gather here to worship, they bathe in its residual miasma. To their conscious mind, nothing has changed. But their subconscious, especially the part that arises from the primitive hindbrain, is far more sensitive. It knows something is wrong, terribly wrong. It perceives what has happened, senses that something else is out there, something not accounted for in the Judeo-Christian mythology that has been rammed down their throats since birth. It realizes that prayers are empty words, cried into an unfeeling void, that no salvation awaits, only damnation for all, no matter who or what is accepted as savior, no matter how they live their lives."

"No! That's not true!"

"It is! And you've felt it too, haven't you, priest."

Father Putney's silence was answer enough.

Oz's tone softened. "But it need not go on, Father. Let me remove that blasphemous object from the window and take it far from here. Your parishioners will return to Saint Lucian's, your parish will revive and thrive. We will both have what we want. What say you, priest?"

Father Putney sobbed. "Take it. Take it back to hell where it belongs."

George saw Oz nod to him.

"You heard him, George. Pry it loose, but don't touch it. Wrap it in your shirt and bring it to me."

George pulled his T-shirt over his head, then edged toward the window . . . toward the Piece.

Roughly the size of a credit card, it still glowed in its place atop St. Lucian's scepter. He'd expected it to be clear but it appeared opaque—at least now. He felt its heat from three feet away. That was going to make it harder to handle.

He went to work on prying it loose, which proved to be easier than he'd expected. The heat from the Piece had softened the lead around it. George merely pried it free with the claw end of the hammer and popped it out into his folded T-shirt. He heard a hiss and saw a puff of steam as it hit the sweaty fabric.

But instead of heat through the fabric, he felt cold, as if the Piece were sucking the heat from his body. He shivered and headed for the stairs.

"Got it!" he shouted.

He found Oz waiting for him in the vestibule.

"To the car. Quickly."

George heard a noise from the nave—a sob—and turned to see Father Putney standing in the aisle, his head down, looking as if he'd lost everything in the world.

George's heart went out to him. He wanted to go to him and touch his shoulder and tell him everything would be all right now, that from here on things would be better for him. But he didn't believe that, and he sensed Father Putney wouldn't believe it either.

So he followed Oz out into the night, into the white moonlight that seemed nowhere near as chaste as it had before he'd entered the church.

3

"Can we shut off the AC and maybe open the windows?" George said as they drove back toward the show.

The Piece sat wrapped in a blanket in the trunk and George had slipped back into his T-shirt. But he found the air-conditioning uncomfortable instead of refreshing.

"Cold?" Oz said.

George nodded. He didn't know if he'd ever feel warm again.

"It happens." He reached out and clapped George's shoulder. "You did well, son. I'm proud of you."

George couldn't say why, but praise from Oz brought welcome warmth.

"What happened back there, Oz?"

"I'm not sure. Perhaps a window opened, perhaps we saw this world through the prism of another. It doesn't matter. It was enough to convince the priest to give us the Piece—to all but beg for us to take it."

"I was glad for that. I thought we'd gone there to steal it."

"I wish to raise as few ripples as possible as we circle the country. We have months and many miles ahead of us. I do not want to be impeded by badge-wearing rubes. We have a schedule to keep, a final place to reach at a certain time. We cannot be late."

"Where's that?"

"You'll see."

"And you need all the Pieces by the time you get there, right?"

"Right. Every last one of them."

"What are they, Oz?"

"Your heritage. Your ancestry. Your future."

"I don't get it."

"You will. You will. That is why I brought you along, George. You still think you're part of them—people like Father Putney and his followers. You're not."

George coiled and uncoiled his left arm in the air between them.

"Think I don't know that?"

"Yes, but they see you as less than they, whereas in truth you are more than they can ever hope to be. Yet you still harbor the vain hope of joining them, of becoming part of their world. But you can't, George. Not because they'll never accept you, but because they don't deserve you. You belong with us, George—with the troupe. We're your family."

George didn't—couldn't—buy that for a second. He didn't want to spend his life in this incestuous knot of freaks. The whole world awaited. He wanted to see it, taste it, touch it. And damn it, he would.

He changed the subject.

"What if the priest had decided he wanted to keep the Piece anyway? Would we have stolen it then?"

Oz nodded. "Of course. Right after I strangled him."

CROCKETT COUNTY, TN

1

"It's not fair," Ginger said, biting her trembling lower lip. She didn't know whether to cry or scream. "I won't do it."

Her uncle had called her to his trailer; she'd expected to find him alone, but someone else was there—that big ugly man with the lank hair who ran the freak show. The one they called Oz.

"I thought you were a trouper," Uncle Joe said, puffing hungrily on his pipe. "You wanted to be in my circus, I got you in, and now the first time something goes wrong, you want to blow the show. What kind of gratitude is that?"

What was wrong with him? This wasn't the Uncle Joe she'd known all her life. Didn't he realize that this wasn't just some tiny mishap? Carlo—her partner, her aerial soul mate—had a broken shoulder. She was devastated and her uncle was treating it like she'd stubbed her toe or something.

The Fugazi family did another series of acts in the show under the name of the Amazing Armanis. Carlo's bit as an Armani was to ride a motorcycle on the highwire. He'd started when he was twelve and could do it with his eyes closed. But last night the front wheel had come loose in mid-wire and he'd fallen, cycle and all. A freak accident . . .

Freak . . . that seemed to be the word of the day. That handsome but sinister character from the freak show, the one called Tarantello, had been hanging around the Fugazi corner of the lot lately, and now her Uncle Joe wanted her to do her act with one of the freaks, that one with the tentacles—Octoman.

"It has nothing to do with gratitude, Uncle Joe. I just don't want to cheapen my act by adding a freak."

"If it's okay with the Fugazis, why shouldn't it be okay with you?"

Ginger was stunned. "Papa Fugazi said okay?"

"Of course—right after I told him what I'm telling you: You do as I say or you'll never work any circus, any-where, ever. And I can back that up. I get it around that you blew my show on the first leg, and no one'll want to risk taking you on."

"Wh—why are you doing this?"

"Because it'll make for a great show. You up there flying through the air toward that guy with no hands— you'll have the crowd on its feet every time."

"But . . . but . . ." She was at a loss for words, desper-ate for some way out. "He's not qualified."

"George Swenson is an excellent athlete," said Ozymandias Prather in his deep voice. "He had a full scholarship to Florida State as a gymnast before the other schools in the conference changed the rules to exclude him."

Ginger felt as if the walls were closing in on her. She looked to her uncle one last time, hoping he'd respond to the plea in her eyes.

"Uncle Joe . . ."

"I've said all I'm going to say on this, Ginger. Now you get over to the Fugazi trailers right away. Oz's man is already there. Papa Fugazi will begin coaching the two of you this afternoon. We've got no time to waste."

Fighting the tears, Ginger turned, stormed out the door, and almost tripped going down the steps. Tarantello, who seemed to be Oz's shadow, was waiting outside. He grabbed her elbow and steadied her as she stumbled. His touch was cold, like death. He smiled. A beatific smile in a pale, handsome face, yet without the slightest trace of warmth. She yanked her arm free and continued on her way.

She stopped a moment later. On her way where?

To her trailer and then home to Momma like a spoiled child? Like a loser? Or grit her teeth and go over to Fugazi country and get on with it?

The show must go on . . . and all the rest of that bullshit.

What had Oz said his name was? George Swenson?

She shuddered at the thought of touching those boneless, fingerless arms. Like touching snakes. But she'd show Uncle Joe and the rest of them. Ginger Cunningham didn't choke.

She smiled to herself. She might throw up, but she didn't choke.

She headed for Fugaziville.

2

"You handled that well," Oz said as Ginger left.

Peabody looked up at him. "You think I was too rough on her?"

"Not at all." Oz glanced at Tarantello as he entered the office trailer. "It's for the good of the show. We all have to make sacrifices. Look at poor Carlo Junior. He broke his shoulder for the show." Oz caught Tarantello's fleeting smile. "The least your niece can do is cooperate with the replacement you've chosen for him."

"Yes," Joseph said, nodding and puffing. "The least she can do."

As Oz led Tarantello out of the office trailer, he lowered his voice and said, "You're sure George will fall for her?"

"Positive. You should see his face when he watches her perform. He's already infatuated. And she loathes him."

"Excellent."

A shame, Oz thought, to have to bring pain to one of his brothers, but George had to learn who was his true family. And speaking of family . . .

"How's Delta?"

"Recovering well. She's tough. We're all tough."

He'd sent Delta Reid—better known as Serena the Snake Girl—to a nearby farm to retrieve a Piece from beneath the barn. Her sinuous shape perfectly suited her to the task. She'd been discovered by the farmer, however, and severely beaten with a rake. But, bruised and bloodied, she'd held onto the Piece.

The day is soon coming, Delta, he thought, when *you* will do the beating and bloodying.

Oz lowered his voice even further. "That farmer . . . do you think he'd provide an addition to your collection?"

Tarantello smiled. "I'm sure I can find something."

"Good. Tonight, after the show, see that he makes a contribution to our Fuel supply."

The thin man nodded. "Will do. And to my collection as well."

Tarantello had the most fascinating collection of body parts. But Oz was interested in what Tarantello would distill from the farmer.

"And when we reach California," Tarantello said, "I may find something for *your* collection."

"I'm counting on it," Oz said.

YELL COUNTY, AR

She was almost used to his touch now.

Ginger remembered how she'd gagged and come within inches of hurling that first time they practiced the catching grips. Not that the freak's skin was slimy or anything. In fact, it was warm and soft and smooth and dry, just like anybody else's. Maybe even better. But the way the ends of his arms coiled and locked about her wrists had filled her with a trapped, manacled feeling that nearly sent her on a screaming run to her trailer.

But almost being used to something didn't mean she looked forward to it. No way. Her gorge didn't rise at his touch anymore but still she hated to get out of bed every morning knowing she'd have to practice with Octoman.

The other performers were giving her a hard time as well. Ginger had crossed one of the lines of the circus world's caste system. There were performers, there were musicians, there were bosses, there were workers, and there were sideshow freaks. Each had its own caste. No one except for musicians mixed between those castes. And even the musicians—the sober ones, at least—steered clear of the freaks. The only outsider who stayed near the freaks was that artist Caniglia with his ever-present sketchpad. He seemed immune to their creepiness.

The dirty looks from the others weren't fair. This wasn't her idea. She hadn't wanted to bring a freak into her act. But none of the other performers seemed to appreciate that it was all her Uncle Joe's doing.

And now because of Uncle Joe she was here on this platform forty feet above the soggy ground, waiting to swing out, do a release, and let the freak catch her. God Almighty, how had she gotten herself into this?

"Please, Ginger," said Papa Fugazi from below. "We haven't got all day."

Okay, okay!

She wanted to scream at them to leave her alone. Just let her be. What did they know about how she felt? She wasn't merely practicing grips now. This wasn't a practice trapeze a few feet above the safety net. This was full height. Sure, the net was still there, but this time she was going to have to hold onto those freaky arms for real—really *hold* onto them. And there were few embraces more intimate than those between people suspended forty feet in the air.

She looked across the void in the freak's direction. Without making eye contact, she nodded.

"Go."

She watched him swing out, build up his arcs, then flip so he was hanging from the bar by his knees. He was good—limber, graceful, excellent timing and balance. If only he had real hands.

Okay, Ginger, she told herself. Now or never.

When his backswing reached its high point, she dropped off her platform and swung toward him. Papa Fugazi had set the trapeze ropes long so that she and the freak practically bumped when they swung together over the middle of the safety net. Ginger matched her arc to his, then reversed herself into the knee-hang position. Nothing fancy here—no flying, no free-fall, no flips or spins or somersaults like she'd been doing with Carlo before the accident. A simple catch and transfer, nothing more. She'd grab his arms, he'd grab hers, then she'd unhook her knees from her bar, and they'd swing in tandem from the freak's trapeze.

Kid's stuff.

"Okay," Papa Fugazi said from below. "On the next swing."

Ginger swallowed, arched her back, and headed into her final swing. The freak was swinging toward her, his arc perfectly timed. She straightened her knees to release them from the bar, reached out her arms as he extended his—

She saw those tapered, fleshy, snakelike things stretching toward her, the tips coiling and uncoiling in anticipation of grasping her—

No!

At the last second her hands pulled back, seemingly of their own accord, and she was falling.

Ginger knew what to do. She'd fallen countless times before. She turned, tucked, and landed on her back in the springy mesh safety net. When she rolled out of the net, Papa Fugazi was there to meet her.

"Ay, what happens?"

"I can't do it," Ginger told him. "I just can't."

She heard a weight hit the net behind her, then saw the freak rolling out and landing on his feet. She turned to him.

"Sorry."

"Yeah. You're sorry." His eyes looked hurt, his voice bitter as he turned and walked away. "What a jerk I was to think this might work."

Ginger suddenly hated herself. She took two steps after him.

"Look, I said I'm sorry."

He whirled on her and now he was all anger.

"That doesn't cut it. *You're* sorry? You've got two normal arms and *you're* sorry?" He held up his tentacles. "How'd you like to grow up with these?"

And suddenly Ginger saw it all. Toys, doorknobs, utensils, appliances, even pencils—nothing recognized his particular deformity. And school—what kind of hell had recess in the schoolyard been for a kid with tentacles instead of hands?

She realized he had a lot more guts than she did, and that she was letting this stupid thing get the best of her. Ginger never had backed down from anything before and she wasn't going to start now.

She forced her own hand to reach out and grab his arm as he turned away again.

"We'll try again."

"Don't do me any favors. I don't need this kind of humiliation."

Now it was her turn to get mad.

"Hey, give me a break, okay? I haven't known you that long and you take some getting used to, in case you haven't noticed. I mean, how long did it take for your folks to get used to you?"

He looked at her and in that instant, in the bleakness of his stare, she saw the answer.

Oh, God. They never did.

"So it's going to take me a while," she said quickly. "One more try. If I screw up again, we call it quits for good."

He hesitated. "Okay. One more try."

Ginger headed back toward her pole and steeled her gut as she climbed. This wasn't going to be easy but damn it she was going to do it.

Nacogdoches County, TX

Oz stood in his tiny kitchen and swirled the rose-colored liquid in the little onyx container, speeding the melting of the last bits of ice. He'd removed it from his freezer an hour ago, but the Fuel was slow to melt. Only he and Tarantello knew the secret of its extraction, a secret they could not share with anyone else. For each aliquot was distilled from a human life.

Oz swirled the liquid again and smiled. Here was all that remained of the Tennessee farmer who had attacked Serena.

He carried the cup to the tiny room at the rear of his trailer. Two pieces of furniture there: a small table and a recliner, crowded among sagging bookshelves. Oz seated himself before the table. Atop it sat a square black wooden platform, two inches high, two feet wide. His collection of Pieces rested in the platform's copper-lined depression.

He was satisfied with the progress of the tour so far. He had eight Pieces now—two of which actually fit together—and that put him almost halfway home.

But collecting the Pieces was only part of the task. The real challenge would be assembling them. He had old photos and even x-rays taken of the Device by his father when the thing had been intact, but its very nature and its link to the Otherness made photographs unreliable.

Oz remembered many times as a boy when he'd sit and stare at the thing for hours. Even in real life, with the Device sitting in front of him, he had not been completely sure what he saw when he'd looked at it. Cock his head this way and it had one shape; cock his head that way and it seemed to change; and as it turned on its stand, parts of it seemed to fade in and out of view—perhaps out of existence. Sometimes it glowed and flashed unearthly colors.

Then his father discovered the truth about the Device—what it could do, what it had already done. He'd tried to destroy it but learned he couldn't. The Device was indestructible. It couldn't be smashed, it couldn't be melted. But it could be disassembled. And so Jacob Prather had taken it apart and made one final tour of the country, scattering its components as he went.

Then he'd killed himself.

But he left behind a journal detailing how he had disposed of the Pieces and what he'd learned about the Device. But not all he had learned. After countless readings Oz reached the conclusion that his father had withheld a secret about the Device, something he felt he could entrust to no one, not even his son.

Or perhaps *especially* not his son.

Oz had tracked down the strange texts his father had mentioned and pored through them until he had found the ultimate secret, the one his father had feared to share: the secret of the Fuel, and what it would enable the Device to do.

The same secret that had terrified Jacob Prather inspired his son Ozymandias.

For him it was an answer . . . *the* answer.

He noticed that the Fuel had completely melted. He dribbled it over the Pieces. The liquid fumed a little, but that was it.

He sighed. Maybe this search was nothing more than a wild hope, a mad fantasy, an exercise in futility.

No. It's too early yet, Oz told himself. I need more Pieces. I need them all.

Bernalillo County, NM

1

They were a hit.

George looked down at the crowd of sweltering New Mexicans fanning themselves with hats and programs and anything else that could make a breeze. But the fanning was automatic. They'd forgotten the heat. George and Ginger had seen to that.

No denying that his tentacle-like arms had something to do with it, as did Ginger's teeny bikini. But the plain truth was he and Ginger were *good*. Especially Ginger. Once she'd gained some confidence in his strength and his timing, once she knew she could rely on him always being there to catch her, she'd cut loose. She'd begun launching herself into great gliding, soaring leaps, dizzying spins, triple and quadruple flips, all with no apparent effort. Even Papa Fugazi was amazed.

And the crowds . . . George knew the crowds were mesmerized. They'd never seen, never *imagined* anything like this. In a matter of weeks George and Ginger had become a star attraction. A beautiful girl, all shapely curves and damn near naked, flying through the air and being caught by a guy with no hands. Even though they still did their act with a safety net, people must have thought it was pretty neat, because the second-night crowds were always bigger than the first—a sure sign of good word of mouth.

The top was packed now. George tried to cap the excitement bubbling in his chest as he stood on the trapeze platform and waited for Ginger to start. To his amazement, he'd found he liked being the focus of the crowd's attention—from a distance. As Octoman in the freak tent, the scrutiny had been too close, the noxious comments too audible. Where he had been passive before, an *object*, here he was an active participant. His deformity heightened the attraction, but what he was *doing* was more important.

And what he was doing was catching Ginger, allowing her to look and be the best that she could, and then being there on the spot, in the precise space-time locus to catch her when she came out of her move. She was so beautiful to watch, George was afraid that sometime in the future, when they did away with the net, he'd become so engrossed in the wonder of her that he'd forget to catch her. And then she'd fall and be hurt or maimed or worse and George would have no alternative but to let go of his own bar and plummet earthward to join her in death.

He'd always thought "hopelessly in love" a cliché, but here he was, in love and hopeless as all hell. And he knew he was being a complete sap about it. He also knew he had to hide his feelings deeper than he'd ever hidden anything before. Because off the trapezes Ginger wanted no part of him.

He could live with that. You don't grow up with a deformity like his without getting used to the idea that there are some things you'll never do, some things you'll never have.

She gave him the nod and they dropped off the platforms and went into their swings. Soon she'd be tumbling through the air toward him. Soon he'd get a chance to touch her, to wrap the ends of his arms around her wrists. Soon he'd feel truly alive for the first time all day.

2

Oz parted the flaps of the main tent and watched George and Ginger do their act. At times it seemed one of them must fall. He hoped it wouldn't be brother George. Oz had set up another kind of fall for Octoman.

He switched his gaze from the gracefully spinning and tumbling aerialists to the rapt crowd of flukum-swilling, corndog-munching, popcorn-crunching, pickup-driving rednecks who took so much of their quotidian existence for granted.

Enjoy it while you can, folks. While you can.

MARICOPA COUNTY, AZ

Atop the trapeze tower, Ginger felt as if she were suffocating. All the heat and sweat from the crowd that had flocked in from Tempe and Phoenix seemed to have settled up here in a moist, ripe cloud.

She rubbed extra resin into her palms. She was perspiring heavily, and from more than just the heat. Tonight, for the first time, she and George were doing their act without a net.

It shouldn't matter, she told herself. And so you shouldn't think about it. Because if you think about it you may hesitate, you may throw your timing off a fraction of a second, and that fraction could mean the difference between a catch and a miss.

Don't think about it.

After all, what was there to think about? They'd already done it so many times without a hitch, in practice and in public, that the presence or absence of the net should mean nothing . . .

Nothing but the difference between life and death.

Ginger readied herself inside and out. As she adjusted the straps on her bikini top she looked across the void at George, waiting for her signal. Everything was going to be fine. She was used to the feel of his handless arms now, and she'd come to have complete trust in his flawless timing.

She nodded to him, he nodded back. Ready.

She swung out, matched her arcs to George's, then began her series of flips. It went smoothly, just as it had all those other nights with the net. She started out simple and built the complexity, from spins to single flips, to double flips, to the big finish—the quadruple flip. She needed a strong swing for the finale—extra height, extra speed. She increased her arc, once, twice—

Some of her sweat had somehow gotten on the bar. An instant before she released into her quadruple she felt her left hand slip and she knew she was dead. Panic squeezed her throat and she made a futile backward grab for the bar, throwing off her timing even further. Out of control, she tumbled upward toward the top canvas. She bit back a scream as gravity reasserted its control and began tugging her toward the floor. If she was going to go, she'd go quietly, not like a howling jackass. The crowd had no such compunctions. She heard it screaming in horror as she plummeted earthward. Ginger spread her arms to slow her fall on the one chance in a million that—

Suddenly a rope coiled around her wrist and nearly yanked her arm out of its socket, and then she was swinging instead of falling and it wasn't a rope it was one of George's hands coiled around her wrist in a death grip—no, a *life* grip—and she looked up and saw his red face and bulging eyes as he strained to maintain his grip. He was hanging by his ankles and must have stretched his body to the breaking point to reach her. But reach her he had and now he was hauling her in. She climbed up his body until she reached the bar, then helped him back to an upright position.

Below, the cheering crowd went berserk with relief and amazement. Yet strangely, Ginger found herself calm. Her hands were shaking and her knees were as boneless as George's arms, but that was the adrenaline. Mentally, emotionally, she was calm. She'd slipped, fallen, almost died. But *almost* was the key word. She was okay. Her partner had saved her. They were a true team now, and something deep within her told her she'd never fall again. She straightened to a standing position on the bar and tugged George along to join her.

"Stand up, George," she said over the joyous tumult rising from the crowd.

"I can't. I'm going to be sick."

"Don't be sick. You're a star. They probably think it was part of the act, the greatest gag they've ever seen. Don't let them down. Wave. Smile. Bow. This is show biz, guy."

George did as he was told, but he looked pale and shaky. Not a trouper. But a good guy. He'd damn near killed himself catching her.

"I almost lost you," he said.

Lost you? What did he mean by that? Did he blame himself? He shouldn't do that. She gripped one of his tentacles and held it aloft for the crowd. The cheers redoubled.

"These things really came in handy today," she told him. "If you'd had hands I don't think you'd have caught me."

"Yeah," he said, finally smiling. "I guess they have their uses."

LOS ANGELES COUNTY, CA

1

After lying awake half the night planning it, George still needed most of the morning to get up the nerve to ask her. When they'd finished checking the ropes and cables for tonight's show, he made sure no one was in earshot, then quickly turned to Ginger.

"Want to go see the town?" he blurted. "You know, Beverly Hills and all that? That is, I mean, if you don't already have plans."

He steeled himself for the inevitable rejection. He just hoped she didn't laugh.

"As a matter of fact, I do have plans," Ginger said.

"Oh. Okay."

Mixed deep within the disappointment was a vague sense of relief. At least his life was holding true to form—no tricks, no curves, no surprises, just straight-ahead frustration.

"Some other time then."

"Sure. But today I'm heading out on the highway and checking into one of those cut-rate executive motels and staying there till show time." Suddenly she turned to him and smiled. "Say. Why don't you come with me? We can split the rent."

George tried to speak but his mouth was as dry as the desert they'd passed through on the way to L.A.

Alone with Ginger . . . in a motel room.

He swallowed. "Uh, yeah. If you're sure you want to."

She gave him a puzzled look. "Why wouldn't I want to save a few bucks? Meet you in front of my trailer in ten minutes."

2

Ginger drove. George sat in the passenger seat and watched the scenery, trying not to let his fantasies run wild. He didn't understand what Ginger was up to, but he was more than willing to follow wherever she led.

He wasn't a virgin. That had ended during his freshman year in Gainesville, thanks to the expert tutelage of the redoubtable Gothzilla—Consuella Marques on the student register. Connie had been a senior and the most outrageous woman on campus.

Overweight, orange hair, black lipstick, lots of leather, and pierced in the most unusual places, she spotted George in mid-September and took him under her wing . . . or rather, under her breasts, under every part of her. She was voracious, insatiable. She taught George all about sex and devised ingenious uses for his tentacles when the rest of him ran out of steam. He'd had no illusions about their relationship. They enjoyed mad couplings, but they weren't a couple. He knew that taking the freshman freak to her bed was just one more way for Connie to thumb her nose at the society she abhorred. George didn't care. He was a horny teenager who none of the girls in high school would even date, let alone allow to first base. College had proven *very* educational.

But soon Connie lost interest in him. And after the gymnastics council changed the conference rules, so did Florida State. He spent years scrounging around until Oz found him. And now he'd found Ginger.

And they were heading for a motel.

They found a Red Roof out near the airport.

"Didn't you bring a change of clothes?" Ginger said as she unlocked the door to their room. She was carrying a blue airline bag.

"Why, uh, no. Should I?"

"You're going to get all cleaned up and then get back into the same clothes? You surprise me."

Cleaned up?

George followed her into the room. He closed the door behind him as she turned on the TV and began playing with the channels. He stood staring at her. God, she was beautiful. That skin, that upturned nose, that fine red-gold hair pulled back in a banana clip, exposing the soft length of her neck. He stepped toward her.

"You can use the shower first," she said, still flipping the channels. "Take your time but don't take *too* long because as soon as you're through I'm going to take a bath, a good long soak." She turned and looked at him. "Well, come on, George. We haven't got all day."

3

The shower was wonderful. Glorious, in fact. George shampooed his hair three times and let the endless supply of hot water run over his skin until he heard the impatient knocking on the door.

"Come on, George," Ginger called. "Save some for me."

He wanted to tell her to come in and *make* him get out, but decided not to risk queering things. He was beginning to have an idea what this was all about.

4

"Doesn't it feel great to be really clean again?" Ginger said when he emerged from the bathroom. "I do this whenever I can afford it. I get so sick of bucket baths. No matter how hard you work at it, you never feel clean."

She squeezed past him into the bathroom.

"What do I do now?"

"Sit in the AC and watch cable TV and enjoy just being alone. When was the last time you were really alone, George?"

He almost said, *I'm always alone*, but thought it might come off too self-pitying.

"See you in an hour," she said and closed the bathroom door behind her.

George flopped back on the bed. He understood the motel trip now. Nothing sexual. Just a chance for a shower, a bath, all the hot water you could use, the opportunity to sit on a real toilet—donniker, as the folks in the show called it—and to be alone. You were never alone in the circus. Always noisy, always somebody yakking a few feet away, always crowded, always something to be done. This motel room was an island of peace and a bastion of simple civilized comforts.

George closed his eyes and reveled in the quiet.

5

"Wake up, sleepy head."

Someone was poking him in the ribs. George opened his eyes. A turbaned Hindu stood over him.

He blinked. It was Ginger, swathed in a terry-cloth robe, a towel wrapped around her hair. Her cheeks glowed red from all the hot water and scrubbing.

She smiled. "I thought you were dead."

"Sorry."

He sat up and rubbed his eyes. How long had he been out? Thank God he didn't have an erection.

"Nothing to be sorry about." She dropped into the chair next to the bed, loosened the towel around her head, and began rubbing her hair dry. "I was thinking while I was in the tub: I don't know a thing about you. Where were you born?"

They talked then. Really talked. He told her about his boyhood in Missouri, his talent for gymnastics, his trophies, his disappointments. Ginger in turn told him about herself, her mother's circus ties, her own history in gymnastics, her determination to get into the circus.

And as she spoke, George realized how comfortable she was with him. Too comfortable. Almost as if he were another girl.

That was it. She didn't think of him as a male, didn't seem to ascribe any sort of gender to him. He was sexless as far as she was concerned. A buddy. A pal. Maybe even a pet?

He should have been hurt, but he wasn't. He was here with her, close to her, alone in a tiny room. He'd have to resign himself to the fact that this was as good as it was going to get. Was it enough?

Yes, he decided, blocking out the dull ache of desire in his pelvis. It was enough. What choice did he have? It had to be enough.

6

"We've got a problem," Tarantello said.

Oz's heart lurched against his chest wall. He stiffened in the easy chair that took up far too much space in the front room of his trailer.

"You couldn't find the Piece?"

But Tarantello's expression showed amusement rather than concern.

"Oh, I found it. It's just . . ."

His expression shifted to perplexed. Tarantello exhibiting uncertainty . . . this did not bode well.

"It's just what?"

"Inside him."

"Who?"

Tarantello opened the door to Oz's trailer and jerked a thumb at the darkness outside.

"Him."

Oz rose and looked. At the foot of his steps stood a hulking shape. A man. In the wash of light from the open door he saw a drooling ugly face with minimal intelligence in his eyes.

"Meet Mr. Spencer Wilkinson," Tarantello drawled. "A man with a country club name but hardly the country club sort."

Oz frowned. "*In* him? How?"

"I couldn't possibly say. But I know it's there. I can feel it."

So could Oz. He could almost see it through his skull, lodged in his brain.

Tarantello said, "I guess how it got in doesn't matter. It has to come out."

Oz didn't think it was so simple.

"I see a problem: He's one of us."

Tarantello turned and stared at Wilkinson. "And your point is . . . ?"

"He's our brother."

Tarantello smiled. "Ah, I see. This is a moral point with you."

Wilkinson could hardly be expected to survive removal. Taking it would be a form of fratricide. Oz couldn't abide the thought.

"We're near a number of medical centers now, and we'll pass others on the tour. Maybe someone, some-where will be able to remove it without harming him."

"And maybe not."

Oz could tell Tarantello did not share his compunction.

"We'll wait and see. Keep him locked up until we know."

CLACKAMAS COUNTY, OR

Oz sighed with relief as Clementine squeezed her doughy girth through the door and exited his trailer. She was gone but her sour effluvium remained, like the refrain from an old song. She refused to bathe. Small wonder why the other members of the troupe disliked her—she was as unpleasant within as without. She might have horns, and a long black face with a white triangle on her forehead, and might perform as *Elsie, the Human Heifer*, but she was anything but contented.

He shook his head. He had enough trouble without dealing with a case of bad attitude. They'd had to pull Janusch from the show after the San Bernadino debacle when he'd been forced to kill to gain a Piece. As an added precaution Oz had had one of the Beagles steal Caniglia's sketches of Janusch—just to be sure. The Bear took the blame, of course. Caniglia would "find" them sometime next week.

Tarantello entered then. He fanned his hand before his face. " Clementine?"

Oz nodded. "The one and only."

"I keep leaving bars of soap on her doorstep but she doesn't get the hint."

"Did you drop off fresh tobacco for Peabody?"

Tarantello grinned. "He sends his thanks. He's totally malleable now. If you suggested driving the circus off the edge of the Grand Canyon, he'd think it was a marvelous idea. Oh, and by the way . . ." He pulled a small onyx container from his pocket and held it up. "Another contribution to the Fuel supply."

"Really. Who?"

"One of the roustabouts got rough with Carmella."

"You took him for a walk?"

He nodded. "When he's missed they'll figure he blew the show. But he didn't. He's right here."

"Excellent. Put it in the freezer with the others. Oh, and how's our friend George doing?"

Tarantello fluttered his hand over his heart. "Hopelessly in love. *Unrequited* love."

"Is there any other kind? How long before he confesses his feelings, do you think?"

"And takes the Big Fall?" Tarantello scratched his head. "Before Chicago, I'd say."

"That soon? No, I think George is shy enough to wait until we get into the Northeast. I'll say Massachusetts. Bet?"

"You're on," Tarantello said.

They shook hands.

SWEETWATER COUNTY, WY

Oz hovered over the tiny table in his back room. The Device was taking shape now. Still a ways to go, but he'd been able to interlock five of the Pieces. He compared the construct seated on the platform before him to one of his father's old photographs. Yes. Some of the larger supporting elements were missing, but it looked right.

Now . . . the test.

He rotated the copper cup, swirling the defrosted Fuel in one of the onyx boxes. He'd forgotten who this was—not that it mattered. It was ready, so he poured it over the assembled Pieces and the loose extras. As he had so many times before, Oz watched the thick liquid coat their surfaces, steaming as it began to evaporate. Once again he was ready for another in a long series of disappointments.

That was why he suspected a trick of the light when a shimmer ran along the edges of the uppermost Piece. He leaned closer. It happened again. Another shimmer . . . and then it spread, rippling down over the others, even the ones not interlocked with the central five, dancing over the bubbling surface of the liquid pooled in the basin of the platform.

A blast of light burst from the Device. Oz squinted into the pale violet glare suffusing the tiny room. Shadows moved around the platform. And then with a soft *pop,* like air rushing to fill a vacuum, the light vanished.

Oz blinked at the Device, at the dried residue of the liquid, and squeezed his fists so tightly his arms trembled to the shoulders.

"Yes!" he hissed. "*Yes!*"

St. Joseph County, IN

1

Gaines—Gerald Gaines on his birth certificate, Esau the Eyeless Seer on the banner over his stall—entered Oz's office. Without being asked he effortlessly found a chair and dropped into it. Gaines had been born without eyes and didn't bother covering his empty sockets. But he'd been compensated for his deformity by the heightened acuity of his other senses.

"You wished to see me?"

"Yes. It's your turn."

"To find one of your Pieces."

"Yes . . . one of *our* Pieces. This one is hidden in a nearby cavern. Retrieving it is a task tailor-made for your talents. The cavern is a tourist attraction so you'll have to enter at night, after it's closed to the public. They have a security guard, and though he's only one man, his presence rules out turning on the overhead lights. Even a flashlight would be risky. But you won't need a flashlight, will you, Gaines."

Gaines smiled. "What's a flashlight?"

Oz laughed.

2

Ginger yawned as she pushed in on the door to her trailer. The crowd that had come out from South Bend tonight had been a little rowdy but wildly enthusiastic. Their response had pumped her up for a while, but now she was just plain tired. Tomorrow would be a lazy day. A motel day. She and George already had the place picked. A long hot soak would do her—

As she stepped in and reached for the light switch, something grabbed her hand and pulled her inside. A scream began in her throat but a hand clamped roughly over her mouth and cut it off. Her trailer door slammed closed as she was pulled to the floor. Then the lights came on.

Two of them—one behind her, gagging her, pinning her arms, the other in front, staring, grinning. Both big, burly, and very drunk. The one in front knelt and popped the snaps on Ginger's cloak. As he spread it he jammed two fingers behind the front strap of her bikini top and ripped it with a sharp downward yank. His grin broadened as her breasts fell free.

"Oh, baby. If you like that freak, you're gonna love us!"

Terror blasted through her. Terror so deep, so powerful it blurred her vision and wrung her intestines. She began to kick and writhe, trying to pull free just long enough to scream.

"I think you'd better quiet her down some, Hank," said the one behind.

"Yeah." Hank cocked his fist.

Suddenly her trailer door opened. Ginger couldn't see who it was but when she saw fleshy tentacles wrap around Hank's throat and right wrist, she knew it could only be George. Then she saw his face, white with fury as he looked down at her over Hank's shoulder. She saw the tentacle around the man's throat tighten, saw his face begin to purple as George dragged his struggling form from the trailer.

Suddenly she was free. The second attacker released his grip and leaped over her in a scrambling dash for the door.

"Hank! Hang on, man! I'm coming!"

Ginger rolled to her feet, rushed to the door and began screaming into the night at the top of her lungs.

"*Hey, rube! Hey, rube!*"

As she continued to scream she saw the second man attack George from the rear, pummeling his ribs and kidneys, knocking George to his knees and forcing him to release his deathgrip on Hank. Hank staggered around then and kicked George in the face. As George went down they both stood over him and began kicking him. But not for long.

Bulky, growling shapes hurtled out of the darkness, leaping through the air, knocking the two attackers to the ground with flying tackles.

The freak roustabouts, the ones they called the Beagle Boys, had arrived. They pounded Hank and the other one into the dirt, then stood over them, growling. Others quickly arrived, nearly everyone from the circus and the freak show who had been within earshot.

Oz pushed his way to the front. He looked at the two attackers, looked at George's bloodied face, then glanced at Ginger. His gaze made her pull her cloak more tightly around her.

Then he turned to the crowd.

"All right," he said in that strange rumbling voice. "Circus people, go on about your business. They attacked one of ours. We'll handle this."

"They were after me," Ginger said.

"Yes." Oz's eyes were not kind as he stared at her. "But it is one of *our* brothers who is bloodied. Go. All of you."

As the circus people straggled away, Dan Nolan brushed by her.

"That's what you get for hanging out with freaks."

She swung on him, her voice a low hiss. "George is *not* a freak!"

Dan's eyes widened with surprise, then narrowed as he jutted his chin toward George. "Well, excuuuuse me. What *is* he then?"

As Ginger watched him swagger away, she wondered at her own words. Of course George was a freak. But she hated to hear anyone call him that. He was a person. A good guy. No one was going to call him a freak within earshot without hearing from her.

She turned back to her attackers who were cowering in the dirt, utterly terrified. It looked like the one called Hank had wet himself. But even a seasoned war veteran might be yammering with fright if surrounded by this group. All the freaks seemed to be there—big, little, one like a snake, one like a tree.

"I hope you have learned a lesson from this," Oz told the two townies. "Never think you can attack one of us. Attack one, you attack us all. And then we *all* strike back. Get up and go. Tarantello will escort you to the edge of the lot."

Ginger noticed a number of the freaks smiling and nudging each other as Tarantello led the two men off. Ginger wanted to protest. From the rage she'd sensed in the freaks, she'd been sure they were going to beat the two men to a pulp. But this was it? A warning and then a walk? It wasn't fair.

3

"The least he could have done was report them to the cops."

They were in the kitchenette of her trailer. Ginger held one ice pack to the squishy lump on the back of George's head while he held a second to his swollen, purpling nose. The easy treatment those two creeps had received still rankled her.

George shook his head. "A walk with Tarantello," he said softly. "I've heard about that. I'm seen as a deserter of sorts, and a first of May to boot, but I've heard whispers about Tarantello. When Oz sends someone on a walk with Tarantello, they don't come back."

"You mean . . .?"

"I'm not sure exactly what they mean, but no one who gets sent on a walk with the T-man is ever seen or heard from again."

A chill rippled across her skin. She wondered what he did . . . then brushed the thought away. Nothing could be too hideous for those two.

Her thoughts turned to George. He sat in one of her kitchenette chairs. From where she stood behind him she could see his bruised scalp. His bloodied shirt was soaking in the sink. She rubbed his bare shoulder with her free hand.

"How's your nose?"

"Broken, I think. Got to be."

"Thank you," she said. "If you hadn't come along . . ."

"T'warn't nothin'. I just happened to be passing by and got a feeling something might be wrong by the way you seemed to *dive* into your trailer."

"But what were you doing out there? Your trailer's on the other side of the lot."

A long pause. Finally George cleared his throat and looked up at her. She might have laughed at his swollen nose if she hadn't known how he'd acquired it.

"I was following you."

"Following me?"

"Yeah. I follow you back to your trailer every night. Just to be sure you get home all right."

Her guardian angel. She was touched. She smoothed his curly hair and looked down at him. He really was handsome, even with a broken nose.

"You're a sweetheart."

She leaned over and kissed him. He returned the kiss. Contact with his lips was electric, awakening something within her. She pulled back for an instant but George stretched up and caught her lips again. She didn't resist. A golden warmth suffused her as she settled onto his lap and slipped her arms around his neck. It all seemed so good and right as her tongue found his.

The touch of his chest hairs against her right nipple shocked her. Then she realized that her cloak had fallen open and they were skin to skin. Suddenly she knew she wanted this good, decent, brave man, wanted him very much. Without breaking the kiss she slipped off the cloak and the torn bikini top, then pressed herself against him.

George groaned with the contact and the ends of his arms encircled her breasts in a soft, teasing caress. Ginger shuddered, not with revulsion but pleasure. It felt so good. And the vague kinkiness of it served only to heighten her excitement.

She found George's belt and began to unbuckle it.

4

Afterward, as they snuggled together on her narrow bed, George was strangely silent. Ginger lifted her head and looked at his troubled face.

"What's wrong?"

He shrugged. "Nothing. Everything. I don't know. This was wonderful, but what comes next? I'm afraid."

"Of what?"

"Of you. Of how you might wake up tomorrow and be disgusted with yourself. And then you'll start to blame me and hate me."

"You got beat up trying to save my life. How could I hate you?"

"Because I'm not exactly a normal person."

"No kidding. And I'm not the brightest or the best educated. I didn't even finish high school. But I'm not a kid and I've been traveling with this circus for a couple of years now. I'm long past the point where I let people take advantage of me. What just happened was my idea. You didn't trick me or seduce me or anything like that. I know who you are and what you are. And I like where I am right now."

She saw tears fill his eyes but they didn't spill over. He swallowed a couple of times before he spoke.

"I want to keep this a secret," he said. "I mean, I'd like to shout it to the world, but you've been hassled enough for being with me in the ring. If they knew about this . . ."

"Yeah," Ginger said, disliking herself for being so relieved. "Maybe that'd be best for now."

The way he was holding his arms struck her as strange. His left was tucked between his flank and the mattress, the right was slipped under the left.

"Are you hiding your arms?"

He shrugged, like a guilty little boy. Ginger knew they were about the same age, but she felt so much older than George, so much worldlier.

"I know you don't like them," he said.

She was stung by memories of how she'd treated him, how she must have made him feel.

You poor guy.

"Didn't," she said, pulling his left arm free and raising it to her lips. "*Didn't.*" She kissed the tip, then dragged it down between her breasts, across her belly, and slipped it between her legs. "Now there's nothing about you I don't like."

She kissed him and they began again.

FREDERICK COUNTY, MD

George was passing Oz's trailer when he noticed the light, a pale, violet glow leaking around the edges of the door, diffusing through the curtains pulled across the windows.

It was late. After the show, when the crowds from Emmitsburg and Gettysburg had gone home and most of the show folk were either asleep or dead drunk, George had sneaked off to Ginger's trailer. Now he was quietly making his way to the freak section of the backyard.

He was beat. He'd have loved to spend the night wrapped in Ginger's arms but that would risk being spotted leaving her door in the morning. And then the tongues would start to wag. A lot of folks guessed there might be something going on between them, but so far he and Ginger had been discreet enough so that nobody could really be sure.

George was allowing himself to get used to the idea that he was happy, happier than at any other time in his life. A scary thing, happiness. Suddenly it just . . . appeared. He hadn't done anything to summon it, and he didn't feel he deserved it, and he didn't know how to keep it. So what was to prevent it from slipping away as quickly and easily and mysteriously as it had come?

It seemed to be slipping away now as he watched those violet flashes from Oz's trailer. Something about them stripped away the warm afterglow of his hours with Ginger, made him forget his fatigue, drew him closer.

He didn't dare knock. Instead he crept around the trailer looking for a window that wasn't blocked, that had an opening big enough to peek through. He found it in the rear corner where a shaft of violet light beamed heavenward through a gap between the sash and the shade. But the gap was a good eight feet off the ground. No way George could get a look through that.

So he watched the light. Something about that particular shade of violet simultaneously attracted and repelled him. And strange the way the color shifted and grayed, as if odd-shaped forms were passing through it.

The light in the church back in Councilville had been redder, but the odd movement within it had been very similar.

George had a feeling of teetering on the edge of some horrific epiphany, that a revelation was near but just beyond his reach.

Abruptly it faded, leaving him blinking and shivering in the darkness. And then he noticed that his tentacles were raised in the air. With no effort on his part, without his consent or knowledge, they had reached toward the light.

Thoroughly shaken he hurried on to his own trailer. The Device and the Pieces his fellow freaks had been collecting along the tour route had something to do with that light. He was certain of it.

He decided he'd better learn a little more about this Device. And soon.

PART THREE
THE HOME RUN

Suffolk County, NY

1

Oz had been surprised to find George standing in the doorway of his trailer. He'd invited him in and they'd talked about how the tour was going, how well his aerial act with Ginger was being received. He looked for signs of distress at mention of the girl but saw none. Perhaps things were going *too* well there. And then George got to what Oz sensed was the real reason for his visit.

"You know the Device you told us about before starting the tour, the instrument you said would change the way the world looks at us? How's that coming along?"

"Very well," Oz said cautiously. "Your brothers and sisters have been remarkably successful in claiming its components. We're progressing steadily toward our day."

"May I . . . may I see it?"

Oz studied him. The troupe had circled three-quarters of the country and, despite the side trips Oz had sent him on, George hadn't shown much interest in anything but the normal he was playing footsy with on the trapeze. Now he wanted to see the Device. What was up?

Well, why not show it to him? Maybe he'd reveal what was on his mind.

"Of course. This way."

Oz unlocked the rear section and ushered George in ahead of him. Not much room leftover with the two of them in here, and no way George could miss the Device. Oz watched the younger man's face as he studied the instrument.

"That's one strange looking contraption," he said softly. "It looks almost . . . familiar. Kind of hard to believe it'll change the world."

"It will, brother. It will."

"But how?"

"Just as I explained: The Device will change the way the world sees us. When our day comes we will no longer be considered freaks. We will be accepted. We will get our due."

Our revenge.

"But how's this weird little thing going to do all that?"

"You must trust me that it will. Of course, if we don't retrieve *all* the components, the Device will be useless. In fact, it will not be a device at all, but little more than a curious construct of peculiar components. And then we won't have our day, and we'll remain freaks and rejects."

George glanced up at him and Oz saw defiance in his eyes, read *Speak for yourself* there.

Oz envied him the confidence that somehow, some way, he was going to make it in this world as it was, make it accept him as *he* was. Oz had never known that feeling of belonging, not for an instant. How could he?

But he craved it.

And he *would* belong. The Device would see to it.

"Is there—?"

He suddenly noticed that George had turned away and was peering at the bookshelf. A special bookshelf. Most of the tomes that lined it were old, some ancient, many of them stolen from the restricted sections of various libraries across the country. George reached up and touched a short leather-bound volume.

Dad's journal!

"Please don't touch those, George. Some of them are very fragile. Have you seen enough?"

"I suppose so. But I still don't understand."

"You will." He clapped George's shoulder in what he hoped was a friendly gesture. "Trust me, you will."

He was going to have to keep an eye on George.

2

Tarantello arrived shortly after George left.

"How's Lover Boy doing?"

Oz shook his head. "Acting strange. I hope this little matchmaking plot of ours doesn't backfire. How did Haman do at the museum?"

They'd set up on the fringe of a small North Shore town called Monroe. Oz had sent the freak with the oddly tinted skin—"The Green Man from Mars!" to the public—on a mission to the Museum of Natural History in Manhattan.

"Fine. Snatched the Piece easily—and helped himself to a few other things as well."

Oz sighed. Another Piece—this one obtained without fuss.

"Good for Haman. Where is it?"

"He wants to play with it a while. I gave him a day if he swore not to lose it. That all right with you?"

Oz didn't like it but he nodded. The Green Man had earned a reward.

"What about Wilkinson? Any decision yet?"

"No. We'll be in Connecticut next week. I've made an appointment for him with a neurosurgeon. We'll see what he has to say."

"And if the news isn't good?"

Oz didn't reply. He had a feeling the news would not be good—no way to remove that Piece from his brain without leaving him a vegetable. And then it would be up to him to decide Wilkinson's fate.

He dreaded the prospect.

New Haven County, CT

1

"I don't like this, George," Ginger whispered as they crept through the darkness.

"Neither do I," he said. "But hang in there. This won't take long."

She didn't understand what had come over George lately. He'd been talking about some sort of device Oz was constructing and how it was supposed to change the world or some such nonsense, and how he had to know more about it. He'd become positively obsessed with it. So when they'd pulled into Ivoryton today, George had positioned his trailer with a full view of Oz's.

Tonight he and Ginger had sat inside for hours with the lights out waiting for the big man to leave. Finally Tarantello came by and the two of them had driven off in the old Town Car. An odd pair: Oz had seemed depressed, Tarantello almost jaunty.

"What if we get caught?" She didn't want to have to take one of those walks with Tarantello.

"We won't if you just stand guard. Will you do that for me?"

"You know I will. But I'm scared."

"So am I. That's why this will be the quickest in-and-out you've ever seen."

They stopped by the front of Oz's trailer. George had a flimsy plastic ruler wrapped in his left tentacle. He slipped it between the door and the jamb and worked it up and down. A few seconds later Ginger heard the latch pop.

"Where'd you learn to do that?"

"After I lost my scholarship I spent some time on the streets of Gainesville. I got *very* hungry. You learn to do what you've got to do." He gestured to the shadows by the corner of the trailer. "Okay. You wait over there. I'll be right back. You know what to do?"

She nodded. She knew: Bang twice on the wall of the trailer if she spotted Oz coming. George would climb out a rear window.

With her nerves stretched as tight as the high wire, she retreated to the shadows and waited. A quiet night. All she heard were the crickets and the constant jingle from the elephants as they pulled on their chains, trying to get free.

2

Oz had left a light on, so George moved in a crouch to keep from casting a shadow on the window shades. He moved straight to the back room.

A lot of strange stuff going down lately. A new, particularly ugly freak referred to only as Wilkinson had been brought on board in California, but had remained locked up with Tarantello. Earlier today George had seen Tarantello load him into a cage in the back of a van and head out toward the woods. When he'd returned the cage was empty.

George entered the tiny room where the Device sat on its stand. It was bigger now, and again he was struck by how familiar it looked. Something from his past . . .

No time for that now. He picked a slim volume from the bookshelf by the x-ray machine, the book Oz had stopped him from examining on his previous visit, and brought it back to the lighted front room. He squatted under the lamp and opened the cover.

A journal, handwritten. On the first page:

> *To my son, Ozymandias*
> *in the hope that he will*
> *someday understand.*
> *And forgive.*
> *Jacob Prather*

George flipped through the pages, pausing here and there when he saw "the contraption" mentioned. Apparently it was something Jacob had discovered in one of the deep shafts during his younger days as a coal miner. He found that people were fascinated by it, so he joined the old Taber & Sons circus and exhibited it as a sideshow attraction. Jacob billed it as "The Mystery Machine" but did not seem to be aware that it served any function.

The occasion of the birth of Jacob's first and only child stopped George cold.

My son, my Ozymandias, is hideously deformed. He is a monster. Martha and I have wept every night since his birth. How did this happen? What can we do for him?

George swallowed. Monster? Oz was a weird-looking duck, but compared to the freaks in his show he looked pretty damn near normal.

He read on as Jacob described his years of searching for the cause of his son's birth defects. Modern medicine offered no answers, so Jacob began looking elsewhere. But along the way he realized that his son's deformity was not an isolated phenomenon. Many people connected with Taber & Son's mud show had given birth to freakish children over the years.

That was a clue. At first Jacob was sure that the answer lay along the tour route, that a "teratogenic influence"—George didn't know what that meant but figured it couldn't be good—would be found at one of the show's stops, perhaps in the water supply. But wouldn't the locals there have produced an extraordinary cluster of freaks? Jacob could find no record of any such cluster.

Jacob came to the conclusion then that the key to the deformities lay *within* the show. His research led him to arcane sources, and in one of those sources he came across a drawing of his own "Mystery Machine."

The handwriting in the journal began to change here, becoming increasingly agitated and difficult to read. George struggled through it.

The story took a bizarre turn. Jacob's search through unorthodox sources revealed that the Device, as his curio was called, was one of the "Seven Infernals" and could provide a link to "the Otherness." Jacob did not quite understand what the Otherness was, but he learned that it existed on the far side of "the Veil" and that the Device was a gateway to the Otherness.

Apparently, Jacob noted, *whoever translated the old texts had a penchant for capitalizing key words.*

When the Device was intact, it maintained a pinhole breach in the Veil, allowing a tiny stream of the Otherness to leak through. According to the texts, that tiny stream had no effect on our world at large.

But Jacob was devastated by the realization that the Device had a terrible effect on unborn children. Every freakish child born by members of the Taber & Sons show—and to people along the tour route—had been exposed in utero to the Device, including his own son. It was all a matter of timing and degree. Brief exposure late in pregnancy resulted in negligible damage, while long exposure during the first few weeks or months yielded hideous deformities, some incompatible with life. Which explained his wife Martha's long series of miscarriages. But during most of her final pregnancy she had skipped the tour and stayed with her mother. As a result their son was born viable but deformed.

My son is a monster and it is all my fault! I can't tell Martha, but perhaps someday I can explain it to Ozymandias. But not before I destroy this Infernal and guarantee that it will cause no further harm.

Jacob went on to describe his unsuccessful efforts to destroy the Device. Finally he dismantled its components and spread them around the country. Ever compulsive about details, he described every hiding place.

Then he said good-bye to his son.

The rest of the pages were blank. George wondered briefly where Jacob was now, but that question was overwhelmed by childhood memories . . . the Taber & Sons circus . . . standing with his mother before the Device, coming back to it again and again, sharing her fascination with it.

He held up his tentacles and stared at them.

She must have stood before it early in her pregnancy when she was carrying him. The exposure had left him with these things in place of hands.

Then it must be true. Jacob Prather wasn't crazy.

He closed his eyes as his throat constricted. If only Mom had been fascinated with the elephants, or the clowns, his life would have been so different.

He shook it off. He'd have never met Ginger. She made up for everything.

But why was Oz reassembling the Device? How was this link to the vaguely described Otherness—whatever that was—going to change the world's perception of the children it had deformed?

George headed for the back room again. Maybe the answer waited there.

3

"Come *on*, George," Ginger whispered to the night.

Despite the August heat she was shivering. What was he *doing* in there?

And then she noticed that the jingling of the elephants' chains had stopped. Suddenly a sound behind her. A growl. She whirled and wanted to scream but the sound choked in her throat. She stumbled back a few steps.

Five hulking shadows, lit only by starlight, emerged from behind the trailer. The freaks known as the Beagle Boys. One of them growled again and made shooing motions. They moved closer, edging her away from the trailer.

The message was clear. *Get out of here. This is Freak-ville.*

How was she going to warn George? These . . . things were between her and the trailer now. She couldn't reach the wall to bang on it.

"I'm looking for George," she said. "You know George—Octoman? He was supposed to meet me around here." She cupped her hands around her mouth and began calling. "George! *George!*"

The growls were many now, and more menacing as the Beagle Boys began to encircle her. Ginger couldn't help it. They terrified her. She ran.

Back in George's trailer, she lifted a corner of a curtain and watched Oz's, waiting for a chance to return. Finally the Beagles wandered off. She opened the door, ready to dash over to warn George, but she slammed it shut again when she saw a tall ungainly figure hurrying toward the trailer.

Oz was returning.

4

A number of the older books were in foreign languages—Latin, Greek, German, and one that seemed to be in some sort of Arabic script—none of any use to George. Finally he found one in English with *Mysteries of the Veil* stamped on its spine. He brought it back to the front room but groaned when he opened it. It was in English, all right, but strange, old-fashioned English that was practically a foreign language.

Suddenly he heard a key in the door lock. In a panic he scrambled along the floor to the far corner of the room and rolled behind the end of the couch. He didn't look up as he heard someone enter and hurry toward the back room. It could be only one person.

From the back room he heard snatches of words and phrases in Oz's unmistakable deep voice—

"Yes! . . . I *thought* that's where you'd fit! . . . Ah! . . . A tragedy you can't be here to witness this, Mr. Wilkinson . . . Now let's see what your Piece can do."

Was he talking to himself?

As George was gathering the nerve to risk sneaking out, Oz suddenly returned to the front room and went to the kitchen. George caught a glimpse of his hands; they looked . . . bloody. He rinsed them, fooled in the refrigerator for a moment, then returned to the rear.

George began to sweat. No two ways about it: Whether he stayed or made a break for it, he was going to get caught. He wondered what the price would be. A walk with Tarantello?

A silent explosion of light from the back room erased all questions.

The same kind of light he'd seen shooting from Oz's window the other night. Violet light, *violent* light that flowed twisting and churning from the back room, alive with shadows and erratic motion.

As the light swirled around George, a roaring grew in his brain, a call, a beckoning. Vast open vistas reaching toward strange horizons filled with mad, groping forms of twisted life flashed in his vision. He feared it even as he hungered for it.

Abandoning all caution, he struggled to rise and then forced his feet to move him across the room. The door was a vague outline ahead of him. He prayed the roaring would mask his exit. Echoing above the sound was Oz's voice, distant, deeper than ever.

"One more Piece. One more Piece and it's done!"

With the thick old book clutched tight against his chest, George slipped through the door and stumbled into the blessed darkness outside.

5

George stood outside Bramble's stall and waited while the last stragglers were shooed from the tent. An old couple lingered, staring at his frozen posture, his body rigid as a tree trunk, tilted at a thirty-degree angle.

He didn't want to be here. He wanted to be reading the book he'd taken from Oz last night, but fate seemed to be conspiring against him. It had taken him a long time to calm down a very upset Ginger who had been sure Oz would catch George. After that he'd tried to read *Mysteries of the Veil* but that old English was tough sledding. He'd gotten through only a few pages before nodding off.

He'd tried again this morning and got a little further, but then it was time to get to his stall for the shows.

But just half an hour ago Oz had come by and told him he had a job for him and Bramble: another Piece.

The *last* Piece.

Bramble's birth certificate said he was John Henry Kobayashi, but he was Bramble to the troupe, and *The Astounding Tree Man* to the public. He'd wanted to bill himself as *Kobayashi – the Living Bonsai*, but Oz had vetoed that, stating none of the yokels they attracted would know a bonsai from a barbell. Bramble's act, if it could be called that, was to sink his feet into a basin of moss-covered dirt and strike a pose.

People would stop and stare at what looked like a man-shaped tree that somebody had dressed in a loin-cloth. Yeah, yeah, so someone got hold of an old tree and carved a head at the top of its trunk. Big deal.

And that was exactly what Bramble looked like. His skin was bark rough and deadwood gray; his arms and legs bent at strange angles; his fingers were too long, too twisted, and too many; his hair stood thick and stiff and kinky, all tangled into, well, a bramble. His features were vaguely Asian—his father had been Japanese, his mother Irish—but his most striking peculiarity were the twigs—or "branchlets," as he called them—that sprouted at odd intervals from his limbs and torso.

So he'd hold his pose, statue still, and let people stop, stare, and move on. When he tired of that pose, he'd assume another. Those present for the realignment invariably yelped in surprise and wonder. The commotion would attract others and soon a crowd would gather, watching, waiting, to be rewarded by . . .

Nothing.

Bramble would wait until they'd dispersed before moving again, causing another outcry, followed by another destined-to-be-disappointed group.

For the moment he held still until the old couple was scooted out, then he straightened and rolled his shoulders.

"That was the *shakan* shape," he said as he extricated his feet from the dirt. For a guy who stood a good six feet, his voice was unexpectedly high-pitched. "It looks simpler than the *moyogi*, but it's more difficult to maintain. The *kengai*, of course, is the toughest. I'll let you know next time I assume *kengai*. You can come see."

"That'd be great," George said. He hadn't the vaguest idea what Bramble was talking about.

"But you didn't come here to learn bonsai culture, I assume."

"Oz wants to see us."

"That so?" His branchlets twitched as he frowned and narrowed his already narrow eyes. "I fear I know what this is about." He looked at George. "A Piece?"

George nodded. "That's what he says."

Oz had given him no information beyond the fact that he wanted George in on the retrieval. George wanted no part but Oz was insisting. He had the option of refusing, but that might get him kicked off the tour. Not many more stops left, but the big carrot of his end-of-tour bonus awaited back in Florida. The bonus was designed to keep folks from blowing the show early. And it worked. Just as it was working on George. He needed that money.

All George could hope for was that this trip would be less nerve-wracking than the last.

Bramble pulled an extra-large yellow dashiki over his head. The branchlets raised tennis-ball bumps beneath the fabric, lumps that wriggled and twitched.

"Lead on, Macduff."

George figured it would be kind of show-offy to tell him that Macbeth really said, "*Lay* on, Macduff," so he . . . led on.

They walked through the deserted top, out the back-door and wound through the starlit backyard. George waved to those he knew. Most waved or called back, but ignored Bramble. George's trapeze act allowed him to straddle the two worlds of performer and freak; Bramble was pure freak.

When they reached Oz's trailer they found him waiting in the doorway.

"Ah, John Henry," he said, smiling as he stepped off the steps. "Glad you could come." He jerked a thumb toward the woods. "Let's go where we'll have a little more privacy, shall we? You too, George. No need to look so glum."

Did it show so much? He wanted to get back to that book.

They walked to the edge of the clearing and stood in a close circle.

"There's a man in a nearby town, a collector of antiquities—mostly religious items—who will not part with the Piece he holds. His name is Charles Eldridge and I've visited him a number of times, most recently last night. I have offered him a good price, but he will not budge. I have explained that it does not belong to him but to us, yet he does not care. He harbors some sort of delusion that I am the devil, or some such nonsense."

"Perhaps he is right," Bramble said.

Oz frowned. "This is not a joking matter, John Henry."

Bramble's lipless mouth twisted. "Perhaps not. And perhaps I wouldn't be making jokes if I—if *we* knew what all this Piece business is about, if you weren't so damn secretive about what you're going to do with these things once you have them all." He held up his seven-fingered right hand. "And don't tell us about justice and acceptance and that crap. Those are just words. I want to know what's going on here."

Me too, thought George, but said nothing. Instead he watched Bramble's branchlets rising and falling— flexing and stretching?—under the dashiki.

Oz said, "And you shall—once I have all the Pieces."

"Why not now?"

"Because I don't want to get hopes up. If I don't collect all the Pieces—*all* of them—any promises I make will be empty. And we've all had enough disappointment in our lives."

George couldn't argue with that.

"You said this was the last Piece."

Oz nodded. "And that makes the success of this little sortie an absolute necessity."

"You're expecting trouble?" Bramble said.

"I sense something in Eldridge," Oz said. "I saw something in his eyes. He has a reason beyond mere acquisitiveness for holding onto that Piece. He's more than a collector, he's an adventurer as well, a student of the arcane who I believe is quite mad. I also believe he knows more than he's letting on . . . maybe something he shouldn't. Or perhaps it's just his madness."

Bramble sighed. "And I suppose you want me to steal it."

"There's no other way. And we both know you can—you're a pro."

George stared at him. Bramble? A thief?

Bramble shook his head. "Those days are done."

"One more time. Consider this your swan song. And I want George to go along."

Me? A burglar? No way.

Before George could speak, Bramble placed a coarse hand on his shoulder.

"Don't take this personally, kid, but I work alone. Always have." He looked at Oz. "You know that."

"Take him," Oz said. "He needs to feel part of the troupe."

George shook his head. "I'm fine. And my feelings aren't hurt."

He didn't want to tag along when he wasn't wanted, and sure as hell didn't want to risk getting caught. Damn that bonus. If he didn't need the money, he'd blow the show with Ginger. But who'd hire a freak and a high-wire performer out there?

Oz ignored him, keeping his gaze fixed on Bramble. "You owe me, John Henry, and I'm calling in my marker."

George saw Bramble's branchlets contract beneath his dashiki, as if balling into angry fists. He seemed about to say no, then put his head back and looked at the stars. The fists relaxed.

"Shit."

My sentiments exactly, George thought.

6

"No hard feelings, kid. I mean about not wanting you along."

George started Oz's car and glanced over at Bramble in the passenger seat.

"None taken. I wouldn't want me along either."

Bramble laughed. "You're all right, kid."

They drove in silence a few minutes, heading across the field toward the nearby town of Monroe. Bramble rambled about how the Emporium stopped here every tour and set up on old man Haskins land, and how he liked the town because it gave him a comfortable feeling, blah-blah-blah.

George held back as long as he could, but finally had to ask: "Oz said you were a pro. A professional thief?"

A nod. "Yeah. Good one too. Second-story man."

"Who always worked alone."

A wry smile. "Not exactly."

He pulled off his dashiki and reached up to his left shoulder. George heard a soft *pop* and saw Bramble wince as he snapped off one of his branchlets. It left a bloody, dime-size pock. He placed the branchlet on the dashboard.

"Sometimes I had help."

It began to move.

More than move. The branchlet walked . . . like a spider . . . like a woody tarantula.

George, fascinated and maybe a little grossed out, watched it scuttle back and forth on the moonlit dashboard.

"Hey!" Bramble yelled.

George looked up and saw the car veering toward the curb. He yanked the wheel and they swerved back onto the straight and narrow.

"It's . . . it's alive?"

"Sort of. I can control them for a while—long as they live, anyways. They need a blood supply, and if they don't reattach in time, they die. I can always grow others, but it saddens me to lose even one. They're almost like children, you know . . . flesh of my flesh, and all that."

"But how—?"

"How did they help? On rare occasions, if I had visual contact and could see what I wanted—and if it was small enough—I'd send one or two in to bring it to me."

"Like a jewel?"

"Never seen a diamond or ruby lying around, kid. But rings, light bracelets, yeah—the branchies were good gofers for those. Mostly I used them to scout out alarm systems before I went in. If a system was too tight or elaborate, I'd pass. One time, though—outside Omaha—I got fooled and wound up in the pokey. The papers had a field day with my looks. Made the front pages at first, then spent a whole week as a fixture on page three. Oz was touring through at the time, spotted one of my photos. Found me a lawyer who got me off on some kind of technicality. Gotta love those technicalities."

George noticed the branchlet's spiderlike runs back and forth across the dash seemed to be slowing.

"So Oz convinced you to go straight?"

"No, two weeks in jail straightened me—scared straight, as the expression goes. The jailbirds they locked me up with beat the crap out of me every day."

"Why?"

"You have to ask? Because I'm me. I'd gathered they were at each others' throats before I showed up. One look at me and suddenly they were best buds, united against the freak." He grinned and patted his bark. "Lucky I'm not thin skinned."

George faked a laugh.

Bramble wasn't buying. "Yeah, I know . . . bad joke."

He pulled out a pair of reading glasses, settled them on his nose, and unfolded the directions Oz had given them.

"Okay, we're almost to Shore Drive. Next right, next left after that, and we're there. Look for number three-sixty-seven."

George made the turn and pointed to the inert branchlet on the dash.

"Looks like he's a goner."

"Not yet."

Bramble snatched it up and replaced its base in the bloody pock he'd plucked it from. It hung limp and motionless. George figured Bramble had been too late, but by the time he'd made the second turn, the thing had perked up and started to move again.

Shore Drive seemed pretty ritzy. George eased along, looking for street numbers. Big waterfront houses—some looked like mansions—looking out over the Long Island Sound. Big and old, with brownstone walls. He saw a brass plaque on a brick gatepost. It read: *Toad Hall.*

He kept rolling. All the places seemed to have well-tended lawns—all except the one they were passing now. No grass, just wildflowers . . . thousands and thousands of wildflowers. Kind of creepy and ugly in the dark, but he bet they looked fabulous in daylight. Fabulous, that is, unless you were a stuffy neighbor. And he bet the area was lousy with stuffed shirts who thought a front yard should look like a billiard table, not a meadow.

Then George spotted *367* on the meadow-lawn's mailbox. He slowed, remembering what Oz had said about the place and its owner.

He's an eccentric, a man who lives in the past. He owns an English manor-style home he refuses to modernize.

George thought maybe he could like this guy.

"Keep going," Bramble said. "We'll park around the next corner."

George pulled to a stop in a splotch of deep shadow under a tree. As he turned off the engine and reached for the door, Bramble grabbed his arm.

"You wait here, George."

"But Oz sent me along to—"

"To what? Back me up? I don't need a bagman. You'll only get in the way. Oz will have his Piece because I will get it for him—but I'll get it alone."

He grabbed the little black doctor bag he'd brought along—"my tool kit," he'd called it. Clad only in his loincloth and sneakers, he stepped out of the car and slipped off into the night.

George felt a pang of uneasiness as he watched him go, but that was leavened by a splash of relief that he wouldn't be risking jail again. He remembered what

Bramble had said about his short stay behind bars and feared he might have an even worse time.

He settled back to wait.

7

Bramble knelt by one of the ground-floor windows, inspecting the hole he'd just cut in the pane.

So far, so good. Oz had said no dog, no sign of an alarm system. But Oz was no expert. Bramble needed a little more assurance.

He snapped off a branchlet from above his right knee—not much pain, no more than a needle prick— and dropped it through the opening.

Closing his eyes, he sensed its "feet" in the tips of his fingers. He sent it skittering across the floor toward the back door, just a few feet to his right. Since the branchlet had no eyes, it couldn't see for him, but it could feel for him. When it reached the molding he sent it up, making it climb along the gap between the door and its frame, over its hinges, up, up, around, and down. No sign of wiring or contacts. That didn't eliminate the possibility of a plunger within the frame. Oz had said the guy was eccentric and lived in the past. Maybe that meant no alarm system at all.

Bramble hoped so. Because the backdoor lock was an old-fashioned skeleton model, probably here since day one when the house was built. A cinch to open, which was why no one used them anymore.

He broke off another branchlet from near his left elbow and fitted two of its six legs into the big keyhole. He angled them and rotated the branchlet counterclockwise. The latch retracted with a satisfying *clink*.

He felt a hit of pride.

Still got it!

Funny how old skills don't die. Like riding a bike.

He waited, listening. No sound from within, no sign that anyone had heard the latch. He returned the branchlet to its home, grasped the knob, but didn't turn it.

He wanted to savor the moment, revel in the pounding of his heart, responding to the adrenaline infusing his bloodstream. He felt more alive at this moment than he had in years. Maybe he shouldn't have given up the boosting life.

Then he remembered his jail experience and decided, yeah, maybe it was a good thing he had. Even worse than his school days back in the Maritimes when all the kids wanted to know if he ever got a woody, or wanted him to bark like a dog. Ha. Ha.

Little fucks.

Finally became so intolerable he dropped out and headed south to Boston where he educated himself. Lots of good libraries in Boston. Did a pretty damn good job too, if he said so himself. And he did. No one else would.

But he had no degree, not even a high school diploma. Hard luck led to petty theft, and that led to a more skilled, systematic level of thievery.

Until he'd gotten nabbed.

Taking a breath, he turned the knob and pushed. As the door swung open he waited for the wail of an alarm. All silent. But that didn't mean a signal wasn't on its way to a monitoring service. He checked the inner surfaces of the doorframe. No plunger. He stepped into a small utility room and ran his flash beam over the rest of the frame. No contacts. A quick check of the walls and ceiling revealed lots of crucifixes and icons, but no motion detectors.

The place was bare naked.

Hard to believe. Like leaving your car unlocked with the motor running.

He could feel life fading from the branchlet he'd sent inside—almost a goner now—so he scooped it up and plugged it back into its old home.

"There you go, little guy," he whispered.

He felt the rootlets sink under his skin, sensed the blood beginning to flow. As it perked up he lost his link to it.

From there he moved through the kitchen and the dining room, allowing only one-second flashes of his penlight to help him find his way past ancient appliances, huge antique oak and walnut furniture, and crosses—big, small, plain, ornate—everywhere.

The high, circular front hall stunned him. He felt as if he'd entered some sort of reliquary. The walls on all sides and winding up the semicircular staircase well were studded with every religious artifact imaginable. Many Christian, but also Hindu and Islamic and Buddhist, and others he couldn't place.

Gave him the creeps. All right: Find this damn Piece and get the hell out of here.

Oz had said it was in a cabinet in the center of the main room to the right of the front hall. Bramble found a pair of massive oak doors. He eased one open and looked around.

He blinked his flash and almost jumped out of his skin, thinking he'd just stepped into a crowd. If the front hall had been a reliquary, this was a museum, a statuary—if there was such a word. He recognized Christian saints, but also numerous Buddhas—or would that be Buddhae?—along with the Hindu pantheon of Ganesha and Shiva and Kali and many, many others. Even a gold-cased Torah on a pedestal. All stood in concentric circles, all facing the ebony cabinet resting in the heart of the room.

Oz had said he hadn't seen the Piece—Eldridge had refused to show it to him—but he'd sensed it in this cabinet. He'd told Bramble he'd be able to sense it too.

But Bramble sensed nothing.

Still, if Oz said it was in there, that was where it had to be. Because Oz knew those sorts of things.

At least he seemed to.

He'd said it was supposed to be the size of a golf ball but was much smaller. Oz hadn't explained, stating simply that he'd know it when he saw it.

Bramble stepped over a coil of rope—what was that doing here?—and started tugging on drawers. Out of habit he began at the bottom in a technique every burglar either learned or was taught: Pull out the bottommost, search it, then leave it open and move to the one above; once that's searched, move up again. Starting at the top necessitated closing one drawer before moving to the one below it. That took effort, took time, and made noise. And with all those closed drawers left behind, you could never be absolutely sure you hadn't missed one. Bottom-up, always.

Some of the drawers were locked. He'd save those for last.

8

George's nape began to tingle. He looked up and around. Was he being watched?

He thought he saw movement in the bushes bordering the nearest house. He watched, waiting to see it again, but the foliage remained still, unstirred by the mild evening breeze.

But he felt . . . watched. That was the best way he could describe it. He stepped out of the car and did a full three-sixty scan but saw nothing.

Still, the feeling persisted.

He got back behind the wheel and was just getting comfortable again when the passenger door flew open. He jumped and yelped in shock as a man leaned in and pointed something at his face. When his eyes focused he found himself looking down the barrel of a snub-nose revolver.

9

Bramble kicked the cabinet. He'd searched all the unlocked drawers and come up empty, then he'd sprung every locked drawer with the same result.

Nada.

"Damn me!"

And then, in that instant, he sensed the presence of the Piece, knew it was here in the room, but not in the cabinet.

"I'm sure you will be," said a voice behind him.

As he whirled, the lights came on, revealing a gaunt, almost cadaverous old man. Eldridge . . . this had to be Eldridge.

He was dressed chin to ankles in a black coverall and wore a black knit cap. A thin scar angled from the center of his forehead down through his left eyebrow, and picked up again on his left cheek. The eyeball in the socket was milky white with no iris, no pupil.

Eldridge wasn't alone. He had a gun, and was pressing its muzzle against George's right temple. The kid's face was dead white, his skin beaded with sweat. He looked ready to pee his pants.

Bramble felt his branchlets go rigid in response to his shock.

"And please don't abuse that cabinet," Eldridge said. "It's more than seven hundred years old."

Bramble raised his hands. "Let's not get carried away here. We didn't come to hurt anyone. We just wanted to—"

"I know *exactly* what you want! Last night, when I rejected Satan's offer a second time, I knew he'd try to steal it."

"Satan?" Bramble said.

"Don't play dumb with me. I thought he'd return himself, but instead he sent two of his deformed worshippers to do his dirty work."

Satan . . . he had to be talking about Oz. Oz had said Eldridge was loony, but Bramble had never expected a complete nut case. Had to find a way to talk him down.

"Look, mister, we don't know what you're talking about. We work for ourselves, not Satan. And think about it: If whoever you talked to last night was really Satan, why couldn't he have just struck you dead then and taken whatever he wanted?"

Eldridge grinned and gestured around at his statues and icons. "Because of these—holy artifacts from all the world's religions, great and small. He was powerless here. That's why he sent you."

This guy had an answer for everything.

"Listen. You've got to—"

"Enough!" He pushed George forward, saying, "Use those blasphemous excuses for hands to tie up your friend. Do a good job. I'll be checking the knots. And don't try anything stupid." He waggled the pistol and pointed to his milky left eye with his free hand. "See this? After I purchased a Dzunabi fetish in the jungles of Borneo—it's now fixed to the rear wall of this room— the village shaman decided he wanted it back. Tried to kill me to get it. Almost succeeded. But I'm here now and he became fertilizer for the jungle. So don't think you're dealing with a timid, harmless old man. Try me and I'll shoot you dead without hesitation, without qualm."

Bramble believed him.

10

Bramble struggled with his bonds but couldn't budge. On his first attempt George had done a crummy job—purposely, he assumed—but, true to his word, Eldridge had checked the knots and found them wanting. He'd clubbed George with his pistol and told him to fix them. Then he'd bound George himself.

So now the two of them sat side by side before the cabinet, looking up at Eldridge as he loomed over them.

"There. That's better."

He slipped his pistol into one pocket and produced a dark blue golf ball from another.

No, not a golf ball. The same size, maybe, but its surface was smooth instead of dimpled, and its color . . . Bramble had never seen that shade of blue.

But the most disturbing thing about it was the way his thumb and forefinger sank into it up to the nail beds.

"Was this what you were looking for?"

Yeah, the thing fit Oz's description, but Bramble wasn't about to admit that to this demento.

"What on Earth is that?" He turned to George who looked scared witless. "Georgie, you ever seen anything the likes of that?"

Not entirely witless. The kid, bless him, shook himself out of his funk and barely missed a beat.

"You kidding? I couldn't even dream up something like that. What is it?"

Eldridge's skin mottled purple and spittle flecked his lips as he screamed, "You both know damned well what it is! And I do too! I know its purpose!"

Bramble turned back to Eldridge. "Well then, you're way ahead of us." Did Eldridge know—really know? Maybe he'd spill it. "What's it for?"

"Don't play stupid with me. You know *exactly* what this is." He thrust it closer. "And so did I the instant I touched it. I found it in a creek bed where I used to fish. When I discovered it was only a fraction as large as it looked—no bigger than an aspirin, really—I knew. It's unnatural. It breaks the laws of God's nature, and that can mean only one thing: It comes from Hell."

Bramble could think of other things it could mean, but the wild light in Eldridge's good eye convinced him to keep them to himself.

"But what's it supposed to *do*?"

Eldridge cooled as quickly as he'd flared. "In the wrong hands—*your* hands—it will bring Satan's realm—*your* realm—to this world! But it was delivered into *my* hands to safeguard from Satan and his minions. I will not fail in that responsibility."

Bramble stifled a groan. This guy's gears were missing a lot of teeth. And he had a gun.

"We don't know anything about Satan, mister. We were just looking for some small stuff we could take off with and hock. I assure you, sir, we wouldn't want anything from Hell."

George chimed in. "No way. We're not interested in Hell."

"Of course you are! Look at you! You're *from* Hell!" He pointed to the tips of George's arms, writhing where they protruded from the coils that bound him. "You! You're demonic! Some sort of sea demon!" He swung on Bramble. "And you! You're not even human! That skin, those hands—don't try to tell me they were designed in Heaven!"

"We're as human as you," George said. "It's just that our genes—"

"You are Hellspawn sent here to steal back this object that your master lost!"

"Hellspawn?" George said, sounding pissed. "I'm from Missouri, for Christsake!"

"Don't you dare take His name in vain! I'll show you! By all that's holy, I'll show you! I'm going to send you back to the Hell you came from!"

He rushed out of the room and returned a few seconds later waving a sword—one of those Japanese models with the long curved blade. He twirled it around like he thought he was Bruce Lee or something.

Kind of laughable until Bramble looked in his eye. What he saw there drove a fist into his bladder.

He's going to kill us.

"This blade was forged by a heathen, but it has been cleansed by holy fire. Now it's fit to do God's work."

George wailed, "You can't be serious!"

"I'm sending the two of you back where you came from. I can't risk my house by using the traditional cleansing fire, so I'll have to settle for second best. Don't worry. I'm not cruel. I'm told decapitation is painless."

Bramble felt his branchlets spasm into tiny frightened fists.

Eldridge's good eyebrow rose as he focused on them.

"What are those? Hands? Little extra hands. How disgusting. How nauseating."

"Don't cut them off!" George said. "Whatever you do, don't cut them off!"

Bramble stared at him. What the hell—?

"Silence!" Eldridge shouted. "You're hardly in a position to make requests or demands."

"But he can't live without them!"

What?

Eldridge stepped closer. "Is that so?" He smiled. "I think I'm going to like this. Doing the Lord's work while whittling a thieving demon into a more human shape. Blessed be His name."

With that he flicked his wrists and the katana dipped. Bramble watched in horror as it sliced through the root of one of his shoulder branchlets. It wasn't the pain, because there was very little of that. It was the act itself, the madness of it, the inhumanity—

He heard George scream, "*No!*" in what sounded like genuine horror.

But Bramble had told him—

Ah. Now he saw it. George wanted him to use the branchlets for something—to untie them, most likely.

Good thinking, Georgie.

Bramble had a better idea. But to implement it he needed lots of branchlets on the loose.

So he cried out in pain and said, "No! Please, no! I'll die!"

No mercy in Eldridge's eye as he smiled and said, "That's the whole idea, demon."

And so the old man began a systematic trimming of the branchlets while Bramble faked agony. The blood leaking from the stumplets was not enough to matter.

He willed the branchlets to conserve their energy by lying still, while he pretended to grow progressively weaker.

Finally, when Eldridge had worked through two dozen or so, Bramble slumped forward, feigning unconsciousness.

"You've killed him!" he heard George cry.

"Not quite. I can see him breathing. But we're almost there. And then it will be your turn. I think it only fitting that I send you home to your master without those demonic appendages. What do you think?"

George wailed, "No, please! Bramble, do something."

Yeah. He'd had enough of this. Time to move—or at least set the branchlets into motion.

He commanded half of them to sprint the short distance to Eldridge's legs—over his shoes, under his coverall cuffs, and up his legs.

Eldridge cried out and jitterbugged away. Must have felt as if he had a herd of tarantulas crawling up his legs. He dropped the sword and began slapping at the lumps beneath the fabric. Bramble felt the blows but they weren't painful and even less effective. He stifled his revulsion at the shared contact with Eldridge's hairless shins and calves, and his even more disgusting thighs.

When all dozen branchlets were in place, he made them stop where they were and set down roots.

This time Eldridge cried out in pain as well as terror.

Bramble straightened and watched the man's panicked eye, his agonized face.

"You removed them from me, Mister Eldridge, now they've got to find a new home. You cut them off from one blood supply, now they must find another."

He glanced at George and saw him staring in horror and wonder. Bramble caught his eye and winked.

"They'll soon bleed you dry, Mister Eldridge."

He guided the second wave up the outside of Eldridge's coveralls—the backside where he couldn't see or feel them.

When they fastened to the back of his neck and throat, Eldridge screamed even louder. He clawed at them, leaving oozing wounds where he tore some free. He tossed them across the room, but no matter—they came scuttling back to climb his clothing again.

"If you cut off these ropes here," Bramble said, "maybe I can help you out."

"Oh, I'll cut something off you, all right," Eldridge shouted as he knelt and retrieved the katana. "Your head! That'll stop them!"

Bramble didn't know how Eldridge had guessed that, but he was right. Without him to control them, the branchlets would drop off and die.

As Eldridge reared up and raised the katana over his head, Bramble began to wriggle away, kicking with his feet and sliding his butt along the floor, but it was hopeless.

Then he spotted one of the branchlets on Eldridge's right shoulder. He leaped it onto the crazy old man's good eye and had it set down roots in its pupil.

Eldridge screeched and dropped the katana as he clutched at his eye. His trembling fingers fluttered over the branchlet as if unsure what to do. After a few seconds of hesitation, he grabbed it and yanked.

His scream was awful to hear. Yes, he had pulled the branchlet free, but his eye had come with it. Blood gushed from the empty socket as he dropped to his knees and jammed his hands over it. The branchlet ran in circles, leaving a bloody spiral as it dragged the eyeball and a trailing remnant of optic nerve around the floor.

As Bramble recalled the other branchlets to put them to work on the knots, he heard George retching.

"No!" Eldridge screamed, reaching a bloody hand into one of his pockets. "You won't win! You'll never win!"

He pulled out the Piece and shoved it into his mouth. Bramble saw his throat work as he swallowed.

11

"Better call Oz," Bramble said. "Tell him we have a situation."

George couldn't take his eyes off the old man lying on the floor, curled into a fetal position as he moaned and cupped his empty eye socket.

The branchlets had freed Bramble who had in turn untied George.

"'Situation'? Is that what you call this? This is no 'situation,' this is a horror show! We're fucked!"

"Easy, Georgie," Bramble said.

How could he be *easy* when he'd just been tied up and threatened with amputation and beheading? His tentacles wouldn't stop quivering.

"What're we going to do? When the cops—"

"We didn't ask for this mess."

"Yeah, but we caused it. If we'd stayed back with the show none of this would have ever happened."

"But it did. I'm gonna call Oz. Drop it in his lap. Let him figure it out."

Wondering how Bramble could stay so cool, George watched him pull out the cell phone Oz had given them—in case of trouble, he'd said.

God, if I'd only known.

Bramble hit a number on the speed dial, then handed it to George. When Oz answered he gave him a quick rundown of all that had happened. Oz listened in silence until the end.

"He swallowed the Piece?"

That's it? George thought. That's your only comment?

"Yeah. But what do we do with him? Bring him in and wait till it comes out the other end?"

Oz laughed. "No, that won't be necessary. I'll send Mister Tarantello. He'll take care of things. This is the last Piece. We can leave nothing to chance."

George wasn't sure he liked the sound of that. Did Oz use Tarantello like Mr. Wolfe in *Pulp Fiction*?

"But—"

"Tie up Mister Eldridge and leave everything else as is. This wasn't how I'd hoped the evening would go, but I suppose we have to take what we're offered. The important thing is that the Piece will soon be reunited with its brethren."

"To do what?" George couldn't help asking. "The old man said if it fell into the wrong hands it could be used to bring Satan's realm to this world. He's crazy, right?"

"Did he mean Hell on Earth? Well, from a certain perspective . . ."

"Yeah?" George said into the lengthening pause. "Go on."

"Never mind. Tie him up and leave. I'll be waiting here." Oz laughed again. "Hell on Earth . . . I like that."

And then he hung up.

12

Oz waited in his trailer, sitting and drumming his fingers. He glanced at the clock: well after midnight. Where was Tarantello?

And then the door opened and a dapper figure stepped through, carrying a black leather sample case.

"What took you so long?"

Tarantello grinned. "I guess I was having too much fun."

"You have the Piece?"

"Of course."

Oz closed his eyes. At last . . . at last he had all of them. He prayed the books were right: That at a certain time, in a certain place, the Device could do what they promised.

Tarantello had his case open. He held up a cobalt golf ball.

"Here is what you seek, I believe."

Oz took it and cradled it in his palm as his brain tried to reconcile how the Piece looked with how it felt.

Tarantello held up an onyx box. "Here is his contribution to the Fuel supply. And last, and possibly least, a little lagniappe, courtesy of Mister Eldridge."

He handed Oz a jar containing a milky eyeball floating in clear liquid.

"Unusual," Oz said. "Thank you."

"You're quite welcome. I already have something similar in my collection, but this . . . *this*." He held up another, somewhat larger container. "Here is something truly unique."

The jar contained another eyeball, but with one of Bramble's branchlets attached to its cornea.

Tarantello fairly glowed with pride. "No one else has one of these."

Oz gazed at the Piece in his hand. "And no one else has one of these. Now all we need do is wait for the right moment." He glanced at the calendar where he had September 21 circled. "And that's not far away. Not far at all."

Cape May County, NJ

1

"I don't know what my uncle is thinking these days," Ginger said.

She stood outside George's trailer and stared at the darkened main top looming under the overcast night sky. The circus seemed to be crumbling around her. Even that artist, Caniglia, had blown the show. They were due in Towson, Maryland tomorrow. Why wasn't anyone striking the canvas?

"I mean, why have we been playing all these one-horse dates in Jersey anyway?"

"Your Uncle Joe hasn't done much more than smoke his pipe since June," George said. "He won't listen to Shuman and Nolan anymore. It's Oz. He's in charge and he's just been killing time until tonight."

"How do you know?"

"It's all in the book."

That book. That damn book. George spent every free waking moment buried in it. Their sex life had dropped to zilch.

"Okay, what's so special about tonight besides being the last day of summer and the day before your birthday? For which, by the way, I've planned something very special. The surprise of your life."

She could barely wait.

He didn't seem to hear. "It's the equinox."

"So?"

"So a lot of weird stuff happens during the equinox. The weirdest thing the world has ever seen could happen during this one."

George seemed bothered by the strangest things lately. He'd made such a big deal about Oz trading in his car and a couple of the trucks for a number of off-road vehicles.

"I'm going to take a look around, see what's going on," George said.

She didn't want to pout but her lower lip seemed to push out on its own. "I thought you were going to stay with me tonight. You'll be twenty-three at midnight and—"

"I'll only be a few minutes."

He gave her a quick kiss and walked off. Thoroughly frustrated, Ginger watched him disappear into the darkness, then went inside. Hard to believe how attached she'd become to George. Just a little over three months ago, after Carlo got hurt, she'd been sickened by the thought of touching him, now she couldn't imagine living without him. She had to snap him out of this.

Because she had a birthday surprise for him.

And the best way she could think of to surprise him was to get naked. Quickly she stripped off her clothes, wishing she were in her own trailer where she could put on something sexy and wait for him. But she was in George's, so buck-naked would have to do. She was just stepping out of her panties when she heard the door open behind her. She whirled.

"Surpri—!"

The word died in her throat. It was Oz.

He towered over her, looking like a scientist staring down at a bug. Ginger turned to run but he caught her arm and roughly pulled her around. She tried to cover herself with her free arm.

"Where is he?" The voice boomed through the room. "Where's my book?"

"Not here!" Her voice sounded so tiny after Oz's. "Let me go!"

"You'll tell me or so help me—!"

He reached for his waist. For a blood-freezing second Ginger thought he was going to unbuckle his belt and visions of being raped by Oz sliced through her mind. But his hand stopped above his belt, at his lowest shirt button. As he undid it he pulled her closer and shoved her hand—her *arm*—into the gap. There was no skin there, just a warm, moist empty space that—

Something hard clamped onto her arm just below the elbow.

She screamed and tried to pull free but she was trapped. How? *How?* She screamed louder and struggled harder as something soft and coarse and very wet squirmed against her forearm, layering it with thick fluid. She retched and looked up at Oz.

Oz said nothing. His eyes were steely, his smile a hard, thin line as he pulled his shirt open, sending the buttons flying in all directions. Fearfully, Ginger lowered her gaze to see what had trapped her arm. She screamed again as the room swam around her.

A mouth. Oh, God, a *mouth!*

There, in Oz's belly, along his waistline, a huge lipless mouth. Thick, heavy, yellow teeth the size of cigarette packs had clamped down on her arm. The huge tongue within licked her hand again, then spit her out.

Ginger tumbled back and sprawled on the thin carpet, only dimly aware of her nakedness. Part of her could think of nothing but wiping the smelly saliva off her arm, while the rest of her would not allow her eyes to turn away from the hideous deformities of Oz's torso.

For the huge mouth was only part of the horror. Above it, just below the breastbone . . . a vague lump that resembled a nose. And above that sat two egg-size eyes—white as eggs, too. So white they could only be blind, but they moved and fixed their blank stare on her.

"No further need for pretense," said the belly mouth in Oz's voice while the normal mouth in the head hung slack and immobile.

Ginger realized that Oz must have spoken through the belly mouth all along, with the head mouth merely lip-synching the words. He stepped closer, towering over her. She tried to crawl away but had nowhere to go.

"I'm not going to hurt you. That would be gratuitous—especially at this juncture. I simply want the book. I noticed it was missing tonight and could think of only one person who might have taken it. Give it to me. *Now!*"

The deafening volume of the last word shattered her nerve. Sobbing, unable to speak, she pointed a trembling finger to the bottom drawer of the bureau to her right. Oz went to it and retrieved the old book. Then he pulled a piece of paper from his pocket and tossed it at her.

"Give that to George. Tell him to meet the rest of us at the bald spot if he wants to witness the remaking of the world."

Then he turned and was gone.

2

George wrapped his arms around Ginger. Her clothes were back on but he felt her shiver and shudder as she told him what had happened.

"But he didn't hurt you? He didn't . . ."

George could barely bring himself to think about it, let alone say it.

"No. Beyond putting my arm in his muh-mouth, he didn't touch me. He said it would be 'gratuitous.' What did he mean by that?"

George understood—perfectly. But how to explain to Ginger?

"He has a machine, the Device, as he calls it, that he's been reconstructing from components retrieved along the route of this tour. Brambles and I found the last Piece back in Long Island. Now he's just been killing time until the equinox, when he can put the Device to work."

"But what's it do?"

"He's been telling us since winter quarters that it's an instrument of change, that it will bring us justice, understanding, acceptance, and compensation, that it will alter the world's perception of us, change our place in the world so that we'll no longer be considered freaks."

"Maybe it's working already," Ginger said, looking up at him and trying a smile. "I don't consider you a freak."

George tightened his hold on her, but even Ginger's warmth and nearness could not ease the cold fear that had been growing within him since he'd begun reading *Mysteries of the Veil.*

"But Oz hasn't been telling us the whole story—or at least not to me. You see, according to Oz's father and the book I took, there's another world, another reality that borders on our own. Borders isn't even the right word—*coexists* is better. We somehow occupy the same space but we can't perceive each other. We're separated from that other place—'the Otherness'—by what the book calls 'the Veil,' some sort of barrier that keeps our two realities from intermingling. The Device can breach that barrier, can create a pinhole between the two realities and let some of the Otherness through."

"Is that bad?"

"I'd say so. Look, almost all of us in the Emporium are a special kind of freak. Our deformities are the result of exposure as fetuses to the Otherness that leaked through the Device. This Otherness is a much older, more dominant, more powerful reality than ours. It changes any of our reality it touches."

"Well then how is that pinhole going to help people understand you?"

"It won't. But Oz isn't planning a pinhole. He has a special substance—the book is vague as to what it is or where he gets it, but it acts as a fuel for the Device. And at the proper time and place, he can cause a permanent rip in the Veil."

Ginger drew back and stared at him. "What will that mean?"

"The Otherness will flood into our world, infiltrate our reality, changing it, overwhelming it until both sides of the Veil are the same."

"Why would he want that?"

"Because then *you'll* be the freaks and *we'll* be the norms."

"But that's awful. I mean, that's horrible! He'd destroy everything? Why?"

George looked away. "You'd have to spend your life on our side of the fence before you could completely understand."

Ginger rose and paced the tiny room in a tight circle.

"What are we *talking* about? The whole thing's *crazy!* Why are you buying into it? Oz is obviously nuts, or he's been dropping acid, or both!"

"Maybe," George said. "But I can't risk him being right. I've got to go find this bald spot."

"Why?" Ginger stepped back and stared at him. "If he's going to make you a normal, why should you want to stop him?"

"Because of you." George rose and faced her. "I'm used to being a freak. I've had a lifetime of practice; you haven't. So I want things to stay as they are. Because with you by my side there's nothing this world can throw at me that I can't handle."

Ginger ran forward and leaped into his arms. She sobbed against his neck, then stepped back.

"I'm going with you."

Try as he might, he couldn't talk her out of it.

BURLINGTON COUNTY, NJ

1

"Are we lost?" Ginger said as she guided the borrowed, aging Honda along the sandy rut that passed for a road in this wilderness.

Twice already they'd become mired in sand. The car's front-wheel drive and George's shoulder against the rear bumper had got them free, but next time they might not be so lucky.

"I'm not sure." George sat in the passenger seat, a map on his lap, one tentacle pinning Oz's instructions, the other curled around a flashlight. "How many miles since that last turn?"

Ginger checked the trip odometer. "Three."

"Keep going till we hit five and a half."

They'd followed the directions up the Garden State Parkway to a state highway, then a county road, then an unlabeled blacktop. With each turn the road had become narrower, the pavement rougher, the surroundings more deserted and desolate until they were now on this sandy path in the middle of a huge nowhere known as the Jersey Pine Barrens.

The night seemed to have congealed around them. So dark. Not even stars above. Ginger never would have thought it possible to feel trapped out in the open like this, but that was what she was feeling now. The overcast sky seemed to press down on them; the scraggly, angular pines lining the road leaned over them like the bars of a cage.

"Turn here!" George said suddenly.

Ginger skidded to a stop, backed up, then swung left onto an even narrower road. She braked to a halt.

"Let's face it, George. We're lost."

George opened his mouth to speak, but leaned forward instead, staring up through the windshield.

"Look."

Lights were moving through the sky, globules of pale fire floating overhead in a line parallel to the path they were on. Heading away. Ginger's mouth went dry as a crawly sensation wormed through her belly.

"This is scary, George. Let's go home."

"You might not have a home to return to if we turn back now. Follow the lights. They seem to know where they're going. Maybe they're headed for the bald spot too."

Reluctantly Ginger put the Honda in gear and headed down the road.

"What's this bald spot anyway?"

"It's what the book calls a 'nexus point.' It's real complicated and I couldn't understand half of it, but from what I gather there are places on Earth where the Veil that separates us from the Otherness comes loose for a little while during the equinox. This bald spot is one of those nexus points."

"Why do they call it the bald spot?"

"Because after being exposed to the Otherness twice a year for who knows how long, nothing grows there. Not even a weed."

Ginger drove on, her sweaty palms slick against the wheel. She drove until she ran out of road, until the path ended in a sandy cul-de-sac. Theirs wasn't the only car here—half a dozen vehicles lined the little clearing. Her headlights flashed across words like Jeep and Isuzu as she swerved to avoid them.

"I guess we're not lost after all," George said. "Those belong to Oz."

Ginger got out and looked around. "Where do we—?"

No need to ask. Behind the trees lay a rise. The globs of light were streaming that way. Many streams, gliding in from every direction, all converging somewhere beyond that rise, a place where pale violet light flashed, silhouetting the gnarled, twisted pines.

She glanced at George. She could see his face in the backwash from the headlights. His eyes were wide, his expression strange. She saw none of the unease creeping through her like a snake. No . . . something else. A yearning.

He looked almost . . . eager.

"Let's go," he said.

He didn't wait for her to agree or disagree. He began walking, shining the flashlight along the narrow sandy path that led through the trees. Ginger hurried after him. They passed through a collection of shanties, recently deserted. Whoever lived here had run off.

Good idea, she thought. If I had half a brain, I'd get out of here too.

The violet flashes grew brighter and more frequent as they trudged up the slope. George didn't say a word the entire trek. It was like he had a one-track mind, like someone had a rope around his neck and was pulling him toward the light.

He stopped dead when he reached the top of the slope. Ginger crept up behind him and peeked around his left side. They'd broken into a clearing atop the rise—a grassy field rimmed with pines that were especially stunted and twisted. She froze when she saw what was happening in the clearing.

Madness.

The only way to describe it . . . madness and chaos. Globs of light swirled and swooped over, around, and through the air above the clearing, dipping in and out of a dome of violet light that flashed and sparked at its center. The dome covered what had to be the bald spot—a roughly circular area devoid of even a hint of vegetation.

And clustered in the center of the spot, at the pulsating heart of the violet light, were Oz and the people from his freak show. The landscape around and behind them didn't match the landscape here. No pines, no grass or underbrush, only a wide flat plain and some sort of mountain range in the distance. The perspective was somehow wrong. It made her dizzy. That wasn't the world she knew. It was someplace else. Someplace . . . other.

The Otherness.

But Ginger's gaze was drawn back to the freaks, all naked, all their awful deformities exposed to the night, all standing in a loose circle around some strange assemblage of odd-shaped parts seated in a shallow tray. That could only be the Device George had told her about. As she watched, Oz tilted a black box and poured a smoky fluid over it.

For a long moment, nothing happened. Then she saw Oz point to the Device and noticed how some of its components had begun to move, rotating at different angles.

And then the dome began to writhe and twist. Tendrils of violet light wormed off its surface and began stretching into the air, along the ground, spreading beyond the border of the bald spot, coiling around the nearby stunted vegetation, engulfing it, changing it.

The dome of Otherness expanded, rising, spreading, following its pathfinding tentacles.

"It's coming this way, George!"

George made no reply, only stood there, staring.

"*George!*"

He shook himself and looked at her. His expression was slack but his eyes were alive, dancing with reflections of violet light.

"It's working," he said softly. "The Device is working. It's widening the gap, tearing the Veil. The Otherness is coming."

Why wasn't he afraid? Why didn't his face show any of the terror ripping through her? What was happening to him?

Ginger glanced again at the bald spot and cried out with alarm at how far the Otherness had spread. It had taken over most of the clearing now, moving to within a dozen feet of them. The trees and vegetation touched by the Otherness were changing, twisting and spreading into new, alien shapes, blossoming with heavy, salivating flowers and spiny, pulsing fruit.

As Ginger watched, a rabbit bolted from its burrow and ran in panicked circles in the violet light. Suddenly something long and thin and white with slavering jaws whipped out of the empty burrow and fastened its teeth on the rabbit's back. The poor creature screamed briefly as it was shaken violently until its neck snapped. Then the white thing dragged its limp and silent meal back to the rabbit's former home.

Without a word, George began walking forward.

"What are you doing?" Ginger cried.

"I've got to go."

She grabbed his arm. "George, you can't go in there!"

"I've got to," he said, shaking her off. "It wants me. And I . . . I want it."

He strode forward, away from her, into the violet light. Ginger started to follow, to try to drag him back, but as she reached into the light she *felt* the Otherness, sensed its alienness, its implacable enmity. Her arm snatched her hand back of its own accord, so violently that she stumbled backward and fell.

She couldn't go into that light, not in a million years.

As she saw the leading edge of the Otherness creep toward her she scrambled to her feet and retreated, screaming George's name, but he gave no sign that he heard her.

2

It wasn't night here. And not like any sort of day George had ever seen.

He stared around in fearful fascination as he scuffed through the blue sand toward Oz and the rest where they stood in the Otherness-equivalent of the bald spot.

The Otherness. It was so much bigger than the reality he knew; the horizon had no curve, seemed so much farther away. The violet light had no source and seemed to radiate from the clear sky. Dim, boulder-rough moons raced across that sky while the clouds stayed low, roaming the endless plain at ground level. Far off to his right a range of sharp-edged ebony mountains stretched into the stratosphere. His own movements seemed slower, the air thicker. This reality felt so much *older*; the incalculable age of the place weighed upon him like a shroud.

And yet as much as he feared it, as much as it repulsed him, a part of him responded to it. Something deep inside knew this place, called it *home*.

Ahead, Oz turned and waved him toward the circle. The huge mouth in his belly mirrored and magnified the smile of welcome on his face. George had wondered at the nature of the "hideous deformity" Jacob Prather had mentioned; and though Ginger had described it, the sight was still a shock.

"George!" the mouth boomed—sound, too, was different here. "You've come to join us. Welcome home!"

Carmella, startlingly beautiful in her nakedness, stepped forward and grabbed his arm, pulled him into the circle. Violet light flashed from her three eyes. They were all there: the Beagle Boys, Delta, Janusch, Bramble, and all the rest. George noticed with a start that Tarantello's groin was smooth as a Ken doll, but forgot that when he spotted Clementine's udder.

And in the center of the circle sat the Device, wreathed in smoke from the fluid pooled at its base. All of Bramble's branchlets were milling around it, alive and well. Maybe they wouldn't need Bramble here.

Oz had an onyx box in his hand. He stepped forward and poured more of the smoking fluid over the Device.

"We're creating a new world from the old one, George. A new world, *our* world, where *we'll* decide what's 'normal.' The tear is small now, but already the Otherness is moving into our old world. Slowly now, but as we extend the tear, its rate of flow will increase. And soon the tear will be irreparable. Then it will be *Genesis*, George. A new Genesis. And this time *we* get to play God."

George turned and looked back the way he had come. He saw footprints—his and the others'—leading this way through the blue sand that stretched on forever. But a few dozen feet away they stopped, as if someone had swept the sand clean of all markings. He saw Otherness-mutated trees and brush, but where were the millions of acres of the Pine Barrens? Where was Ginger?

Ginger!

The memory of her came like a splash of icy water in the face. She was out there somewhere, terrified—for herself, but mostly for him. For *him.*

And what was he feeling for her?

Part of him wanted Oz and the rest to have their way. These people—deformed like him, outcasts like him— they'd taken him in and made him part of their family when everyone else had discarded him. They wanted this.

And damn it, he wanted it too. Or at least that part of him did. Another part wanted to be back with Ginger, wanted to protect her from the horror that the Otherness would make of her daily existence.

And yet . . . he felt he *belonged* here. He held up his tentacles and stared at them, coiling and uncoiling before his face. Not to have to hide them, to *flaunt* them instead. What would that be like?

No. It wasn't enough. The belonging he sensed here couldn't replace how he felt with Ginger. Nothing the Otherness could offer would ever top that.

George turned again toward the Device. Oz had just finished emptying the contents of still another onyx box over it. Without allowing himself to think, without giving himself a chance to change his mind, George made two quick steps into the center of the circle and booted the Device, putting all the force he could muster behind the kick.

Pain shot up his leg as pieces of the Device were knocked loose and sent flying, tumbling through the air in a dozen directions. Shouts of shock and rage rose on all sides as bolts of light—white, pure light—flashed from the damaged Device and arced into the sky. A wind began to blow, swirling the sand into stinging blue vortices.

"The tear!" Oz shouted. "It's closing! Everything's being undone. Find those Pieces and bring them to me!"

Not enough, George realized. Not enough merely to knock the Pieces loose. Oz could simply reassemble them. George had to bury them, scatter them where they couldn't find them.

Or better yet, put one beyond their reach. Just one. The Device was useless if it was incomplete.

George spotted a Piece at his feet. He wrapped one of his tentacles around it and ran. Back. Back along the way he'd come. He squinted against the swirling sand, trying to stay on course, but the gusts had filled and smoothed his tracks. Ahead of him the air shimmered and flashed with darkness, while behind him George heard baying howls from the Beagle Boys as they took up the chase.

He kicked up his speed. If they got hold of him, who knew what they might do?

3

The steady advance of the violet light of the Otherness had backed Ginger over the edge of the rise, and now she was retreating down the slope.

She sobbed with every backward step. George had left her, deserted her for the other freaks. She'd seen the way he'd let Carmella take his hand and lead him into that circle. And now the Otherness was coming, changing everything, taking over—

Then she noticed a change in the violet light. Its questing tendrils withdrew as its leading edge flickered and began to pull back. Hesitantly, she followed its retreat. When she regained the top of the rise she could see the clearing again, still within the shrinking dome of violet light. But the light had a grainy, ground-glass appearance. She thought she saw a shadow moving within—a number of shadows.

Suddenly a figure burst from the violet light and came bounding across the clearing toward her, running as if the hounds of Hell were on his tail.

"George!"

His features were dim in the violet glow, but his expression was frightened, desperate. Without a word he pushed her back into the shadowy brush at the edge of the clearing and thrust something into her hand.

"Hide here. Don't move. Don't make a sound no matter what happens. I'll be okay. I'll be back for you."

Then he kissed her and ran down the slope.

No sooner had he been swallowed by the darkness than five hulking, growling forms burst from the steadily shrinking light and pursued him. Moments later they returned, dragging him along in their midst.

Ginger locked a scream in her throat and fought the urge to rush to his aid. He'd told her to stay hidden. And besides, what could she do? She'd be swatted like a fly. So she huddled in the brush and watched the Beagle Boys hustle George back into the Otherness.

. . . I'll be okay . . . I'll be back for you . . .

Only those words kept her from screaming out the insufferable fear that she'd never see him again.

Vaguely through the swirling violet light she could make out the circle of freaks in the bald spot. They seemed to be searching the ground for something. When George was brought back to them they searched him, then began beating him. Finally they pushed him aside and resumed sifting the sand around them.

Ginger held up the thing in her hand. It felt cold and fuzzy, almost furry. Was this what they were searching for?

When she looked up again she was startled at how small the violet dome had become, how quickly its light was fading. Panic tightened its fist within her chest. What was happening? And what would happen to anyone caught inside if and when it faded completely? She dropped the Piece and ran forward.

"George!"

She spotted him. He staggered to his feet and stared around. He looked lost. She shouted his name but he gave no sign that he heard. She *screamed* his name. The dome was shrinking so *fast!*

Maybe he heard her, maybe it was some sort of instinct. Whatever the reason, he began to stumble in her direction. The others didn't seem to notice. They were still searching through the sand around the Device. But George seemed to be moving in slow motion, tilted forward, head down, as if fighting a gale. His tentacles were stretched out straight and stiff before him, blindly reaching toward her.

Still calling his name, Ginger inched up to the receding edge of the light and thrust her hand within. The enmity, the alienness coursed through her but she forced her hand farther in. It was cold in there and she felt the blast of the wind, the sting of the sand. She pushed her arm still deeper into the light, up to the shoulder, stretched and managed to touch the tip of George's right tentacle. It responded immediately to her touch, writhing through her palm and wrapping around her wrist in the catch grip they'd used so many hundreds of times in mid air.

George looked up and smiled, though she knew he couldn't see her. He said something she couldn't hear but she read his lips.

Pull!

Ginger planted her feet and leaned back, trying to haul him through, but the drag was too strong. She was losing ground, especially now that the dome was shrinking faster—*collapsing.*

Her feet began sliding through the sandy soil. Instead of pulling George out, she was being pulled in. She dropped to her knees and with her free hand grabbed a gnarled dead root looping out of the soil. It stopped her slide, and for a moment she thought she was going to win. But the pull was too great. Her fingers slipped free of the root and once more she was heading into the violet light.

George must have realized this. He began wriggling his tentacle free of her grasp.

"No!" she cried. "Don't let go! I'll get you out!"

He shook his head and his lips formed a firm *No.* He touched his free tentacle to his lips then pressed it against the back of her hand.

"Please, George! Don't let me go!" She tried desperately to keep a grip on him but his flesh was so loose and flexible that he managed to slip free. "George, *no!*"

But he was going, sliding backward toward the bald spot and the others within it. He waved. He looked like he was crying.

And then George was gone. Everything was gone. A loud bang, like a giant balloon exploding, and suddenly the light, the Otherness, Oz, the freaks, George— everything. Gone.

Gone!

"Oh, no! Oh, please, God—*NO!*"

Sobbing, crying, refusing to believe this was real, Ginger ran forward into the bald spot and staggered around in blind circles, screaming out George's name until her throat was raw and her voice torn and useless. But no answer came. Even the night insects were quiet. Only the cold eye of the moon in the clearing sky bore witness to what had happened here.

She dropped to her knees. George . . . gone . . . lost inside the Otherness . . . maybe even dead now . . .

And what time was it? Had to be after midnight. George's birthday. His present . . . his birthday surprise . . . she hadn't been able to tell him about it . . . he'd been taken from her before she'd had a chance to tell him about their baby.

END

Made in the USA